MAYAN BLUE

MICHELLE GARZA
MELISSA LASON

Sinister Grin Press

MMXVI

Austin, Texas

Sinister Grin Press

Austin, TX

www.sinistergrinpress.com

May 2016

Cover Art by Zach McCain

Book Design by Travis Tarpley

Edited by Erin Sweet-Al Mehairi

ISBN: 978-1-944044-21-3

DEDICATION

This book is dedicated to my father in law Garry Lason. His love and pride in me kept me going even when my faith in myself was shaky. May he rest in peace always. Also to my husband Chris Lason who gave me a typewriter when we were young and always pushed me to follow my dreams. Our beautiful miracle Kahlan Olivia who keeps mommy on her toes and already loves books. And of course my family the Wax and Lason clans for your love and support you never let me down. Finally, to all my friends who give me some much support that is greatly appreciated. – Melissa Lason

I would like to thank my husband, Ricky, and my two little boys for being there for me and filling my life with love. My mom for showing me my first horror movies and reading to me, my dad for telling me scary stories around the campfire-you both sparked my interest in becoming a storyteller. I would also like to thank my family for always supporting and encouraging me. A big thank you to our friends that have become our horror family, much love to you all! - Michelle Garza

PROLOGUE

The priestess drew an ornate, obsidian dagger. The workers, mere boys, stepped forward without hesitation. From their backs blasted a cold wind, nearly snuffing the torches in their blistered hands, and leaving the scent of decay filling the cramped space around them. Beyond the tiny chamber in which they worked was an expansive cavern, a place of death. The skin of the priestess had been painted a brilliant blue, which raised goose bumps upon the young men's arms, turning their insides cold with finality for they too had been anointed with the same pigment. She nodded, signaling them to leave their torches on the damp floor and to raise a disc into its place in the center of a set of large, stone doors. The opposite side of the doors had been beautifully carved, along with the elaborate disc, by the hands of the boys' fathers, who were the last of the men to be taken. The circular seal had been intricately etched with the story of their end, serving as a warning. It expended every ounce of their combined strength to push the doors closed before them. Mortar was filled in around the disc, closing the antechamber off forever. The boys stepped away as the priestess began her incantation. She fought to keep her voice strong and to not betray the dread dwelling within her heart. Her young companions knelt before her and the sight of them waiting to die brought sadness to her spirit. She lifted the blade, and her voice rose into a commanding chant of one beseeching the gods to answer her. An offering of blood was the way of her people. She cut the first boy's throat and his blood spilled over her hands in a warm rush. He took it solemnly; his father would have been proud of his bravery. The second went just as silently and there was not an ounce of fear in his face as she pulled the dagger across his throat. Blood pooled around their pale-faced corpses as she finished her prayer. Behind her radiated the energy of pure malice, its maw set wide open to devour her before the rite was complete. The priestess couldn't allow it victory as it had claimed far too many already. With self-sacrifice, there was no greater an offering. She brought the blade down into the side of her abdomen in a quick, brutal jab, and it stole her breath in an instant. She dragged the incision out wide, opening herself up before the doors. Hot blood sprayed upon the cold stone before coursing down her legs. Her voice became ragged wailing as she begged the ancient ones to seal the entryway before her, along with the lands of fear behind her, in order to spare the handful of her people still living. Her offering, coupled with the blood of the two boys, went racing up the doors like crimson vines, twining across the entire surface. Her abdomen fell open, emptying her vital organs upon the damp cave floor. She fell to her knees as a second blast of wind buffeted her with the cries of defeat issuing from the lands of death, and then, a white pulse like a single burst of lightning illuminated her failing body. Her prayer ceased along with the beating of her heart.

CHAPTER ONE

The caverns had not been touched by the presence of man in centuries, but the professor could not shake the feeling he wasn't alone. He had felt this sensation before many times in his days in the field. He questioned himself for not waiting for Wes as going into caves alone was really against protocol. Yet with his age had come some overconfidence. He excavated many tombs in South America and Mexico and each time the atmosphere was much the same. His heart beat with excitement, knowing he was on the brink of something major. The professor's helmet lantern cast a yellow circle around him as he explored the underground labyrinths, and at times, it felt hard to breathe as the stone walls crept closer and closer to him. Yet, he would not yield to the anxiety of false suffocation. After hours of traversing those dark caverns alone, marking his trail with white chalk, he found himself standing triumphantly before a set of elaborate stone doors. He raised a trembling hand to trace the markings of a disc set in the center of them, while marveling at the carvings. Their existence was a ghost he had been chasing for many years. Around the circular seam he could see the mortar was weakening, which caused his better judgment to soon begin to crumble as well. He lowered his backpack to the floor, which contained many of his smaller archaeological tools, but nothing strong enough to pry free an entire stone door. He had to figure something else out, and then quietly the disc called out to him. He unzipped his pack, grabbed his hand pick, spun it in the light of his headlamp, then eased it into the eroded circular seam. He claimed the disc to show to the rookie professor when they met up to prove the old man's wildest hypothesis.

****

Alissa turned the radio on just to avoid Kelly's line of questioning. It was true she had a crush on the associate professor and the prodding by her horny dormmate only made it worse. She just hoped Kelly would keep her mouth shut about it while Wes was around. Wes was in charge of their group and allegations of any fooling around with students could ruin his career. He drove them for hours speaking primarily about professor Lipton, which made it clear Wes was very passionate about his work. Alissa didn't want to sully his reputation as being a great young instructor, but she did find him irresistible.

"Turn that shit up while they are gone. We have been stuck in this van all damn day with him crying about that crazy old bastard. I need to hear some tunes," said Kelly as she held a small mirror up to her face, checking her makeup, and combing her fingers through her straight, blonde hair.

"That's pretty insensitive, seeing as how he is the one paying for this trip, so why did you come anyway?" Alissa asked silencing the radio. "If you're going to be a bitch, you should've stayed back in your dorm."

Kelly rolled her eyes, and then nodded to the three approaching the van. "Two of them are fuckable, sweetheart. You can play your flirty teen girl act with that other douchebag, but Dennis and Tyler are fine and both come from rich families!"

Alissa sighed, "You could've played this game back on campus and spared us your princess bullshit."

Kelly shook her head, "Don't be jealous, Alissa. It's not my fault that guys only want to be your buddy and nothing else. I can't help it that they all want me!"

Alissa didn't want to admit to herself the comment was partially true. She looked at herself in the rearview mirror: mousy, brown hair and thick-framed glasses. Her body was not as sleek as the girl who sat primping herself in the seat next to her.

"Wow, you base your self-worth on how many guys want to bone you, so you're right, I am so jealous I could shit!"

Kelly playfully slapped Alissa's shoulder from the back seat, "You're so gross! I can't believe you sometimes!"

Alissa's line of defense was always the same--to play it off like she didn't care what people thought about her, but sometimes she did wonder why some girls had it so easy, while she was doomed to be less attractive and socially awkward.

Dennis opened the van door and jumped in beside Kelly.

"Ladies, we brought you something for the road."

Tyler handed Kelly a diet soda and a granola bar as he opened the door on the other side of her. He tossed a root beer and a bag of potato chips to Alissa. The difference was obvious to both women in the way he gently handed Kelly her food, but threw Alissa hers as if touching her skin would infect him with a contagious disease. She pulled the bag open and held it between her thighs, shoving the barbecue-flavored chips into her mouth to stop it from asking him why he was such a dick. *I don't even like barbecue chips, asshole. I wanted Cheetos and Mountain Dew, but you damn sure found exactly what the princess wanted didn't you, fuckin prick?*

Wes climbed into the driver's seat, and then pulled back out onto the mountain road before continuing northward. Kelly bitched at Alissa until she found a radio station Kelly could screech along to, while she bounced about in the seat. Alissa knew it was all a show for the two dominant males in the back seat beside her. Kelly was your typical rich girl. Her daddy was paying for her to become a high school teacher even though she planned to be married into money before she ever really began her career. Tyler and Dennis were over-tanned, yuppie types and both were in supreme shape, though Tyler was a bit more muscular due to his years playing football. Wes had pale skin, black hair, and a shy personality, plus he was ten years older than Alissa, which only made him more mature and far more appealing to her. The excursion was funded by Wes and Professor Lipton and the group was supposed to meet the professor at the base of Brasstown Bald Mountain to assist in the recovery of what he claimed could be an artifact that proved his speculations. Alissa looked to Wes in confusion when he drove right by their exit. She had mapped it out on the GPS on her cell phone. Wes glanced over to her and winked, so she eased back into the seat.

"You know where we're going right?" Kelly questioned, "I don't want to get lost up here with all the crazy cannibal hillbillies!"

"Come on, Kelly!" Alissa scolded, glancing into the rear-view mirror. Alissa watched Wes's face, but it was blank except his eyes registering something else.

"Almost there," he said as his voice shook with anticipation.

"That's good," said Kelly as she unbuckled her seatbelt, "cuz I only brought enough supplies to last a week!" From her tote bag, Kelly pulled a bottle of whiskey and a bag that Alissa knew was probably the last of her own stash.

"I told you to leave that shit back in the dorm," said Alissa. She didn't want Wes losing his job over something so stupid. She had been trying to make a connection with him since the previous semester. She wanted to show him she wasn't the typical college floozy and that she was different from girls like Kelly.

"I didn't see anything," Wes said. He smiled, but Alissa could see apprehension in his eyes.

"It's just a little weed, come on. You're such a downer, Alissa!" said Tyler, as he grabbed the bag and sniffed it. "Smells fuckin great, Kell!" He used the nickname that always turned Alissa's guts, but her envy was quelled by almost laughing out loud, biting back the response she wished she could scream in his face.

"That's not Kell's weed, it's mine, I hope you like the smell of my hippie brother's underwear by the way, cuz that's where he hid the shit, right under his nut sack while he drove across three states. It's all saturated in sweat, pubes, and vegan farts!"

Dennis went for the bottle and said, "Alright! No cheap shit here. I'm gonna show you guys how to get tore up!" He held it up to his mouth, then with exaggeration pretended to swig the whole thing. Kelly's giggle stung Alissa like a paper cut. She wondered if she would be able to handle the next week of being in such close company with the prom queen and the two cavemen.

****

They drove the back roads for hours until they reached a dead end, the point where it was time to "hoof it" as Wes said and they left the white van parked beneath a tree. He pulled a map from his pack to study it momentarily.

"Our cell phones won't work out here, so let's bag them up. Lipton has my GPS so we have to do it old school style until we meet up with him." Wes said.

"Have no fear, I know what I'm doing... I think," he teased.

"Alright, let's go!" Alissa smiled. Her excitement sounded a little over- exaggerated causing her to cringe at her own voice.

Wes had been with Professor Lipton on a few minor excursions and he was confident the old man was on to something big. Recently the professor had made a rubbing of a carved stone he thought linked the Mayans to a settlement near Brasstown Bald Mountain. The old man swore it was a map leading to another location closer to Blood Mountain. Professor Lipton survived cancer, his thirst for life renewed. He told Wesley he had never felt stronger or more alive and he was ready to prove his claim that the Mayans had settled in Georgia.

Alissa walked beside him in silence as his mind wandered through memories. The other three trailed behind, their voices echoing through the silent hills.

"I wish they would shut up, maybe we would see some wildlife!" Alissa said as she glanced back over her shoulder, glaring at Kelly.

"I'll show you some wildlife!" Kelly said pulling off her shirt and then continuing to walk in only her sports bra and shorts.

"Hell yeah!" Dennis cheered and then did the same, his chest shaved bare.

Alissa was sickened by how cliché it all was, a display of pure college jock manliness. Her only salvation in the next seven days would be Wesley who walked as quiet as a mouse beside her. She knew the reason why he needed the two cavemen behind them, there was no way they could possibly carry any artifacts back to the van if it was just the two of them. Kelly invited herself just to decide which of the two best friends would be her ninth boyfriend of the year.

"Ok, so if we don't find this thing or even the professor, does this still count as extra credit?" Tyler asked, chewing on a half-melted energy bar from his backpack.

"We already signed off on it, Tyler. Even if we came back with nothing but a hangover, you'll still get the credit," Wes mused.

"Fuck yeah bro, that's why I like you. You're not like those other little pansies, you're cool under all that geeky shit!"

Wes shook his head, smiling a crooked smile, which turned Alissa's cheeks red.

"I feel lucky to have such an opportunity," she said.

"I can't believe Dean Reynolds agreed to this," Tyler said.

"I think the dean felt sorry for Professor Lipton and agreed to grant credit for this crazy expedition. You know, with him being sick and all," Kelly said.

Alissa shot her a look of death to silence Kelly's inconsiderate blabbering. The blonde rolled her eyes in response.

"The professor has had some health problems, but the dean allowed this trip only because he believes in Professor Lipton, even though others may not," Wes answered.

"Well, I'm basically here as a volunteer, but the rest of you guys sure got the hook up!" Kelly whined. "Bunch of fuckin' brainiacs."

Alissa shook her head. It was true Kelly wouldn't be granted credit, but her motivation was far from just being a volunteer. Alissa was studying anthropology, while Dennis and Tyler were going for degrees in history. Both were actually smart beneath their bonehead behavior, though they rarely showed it.

****

They stopped in the evening to make camp, each unrolling their sleeping bags then popping them out. Alissa brought along her brother's pop-up two-person tent, which was just big enough to sleep in, plus it provided the girls with a little added protection from the elements.

"Hey, that looks like a tight fit, are you two gonna get on top of each other or what?" Tyler asked.

"Where's your tent?" Kelly asked.

"We're men, honey. We don't need a tent," Tyler said flexing his muscular arms. "But if you're inviting me in, I won't say no."

"Don't start your stupid shit again!" Alissa said.

She was attempting to eat some sort of dehydrated dinner. It was advertised as being macaroni and cheese, but it tasted like sand. She was in no mood for his innuendoes.

"Take it easy!" he said, then pulled out the bottle of liquor. "Maybe this will loosen you up a little bit."

He screwed off the lid, and then he held it down to her. Alissa took it and hit it hard, before smirking when he wiped it clean with his shirt to offer it to Kelly.

"Let's get this party started!" the blonde giggled, downing the whiskey while pulling her hair free from a ponytail. It fell lightly about her tan shoulders. She danced around the fire, swaying her hips.

"Didn't anyone bring some music?"

Her two admirers rummaged through their backpacks in a frenzy. Dennis found his first, jumping up and holding it above his head in victory.

"I got it, I got it, Kell!"

He hooked his mp3 player up to a set of mini-speakers and began blasting horrid club music which made Alissa cringe internally.

"Not too loud, I'm trying to unwind," Wes scolded.

"Well, maybe this will help!" Tyler smiled, digging his fingers in the bag of weed. Wes only shook his dark hair, sighing as he moved to the perimeter of the camp to sit on a fallen tree, his eyes searching the endless miles of forest.

Kelly kept on dancing, and Tyler and Dennis thought it was quite seductive. Alissa thought she looked more like a cheap stripper. Kelly straddled Dennis who sat on a log and Alissa rolled her eyes as her dormmate began giving her potential suitor a lap dance.

"Me next!!!" Tyler hollered as he finished rolling a joint. "Where's my one dollar bills?" he joked, patting his pocket with his free hand.

23

"Better be higher denominations than that or I'll shake this ass somewhere else!" Kelly sulked in mock offense before climbing off of Dennis to stand in front of Tyler to continue her show.

Clouds began to form as they set up camp and it soon became clear a storm was about to cut loose. Winds whipped through the small fire sending embers scattering out into the trees surrounding them.

"The weather report said it would be clear all weekend," said Wes quizzically.

"Holy shit!" Kelly giggled.

The alcohol was taking a hold of her as she stumbled against the storm.

"Get in the tent!" Alissa yelled over the wind

"What about us?" Tyler asked. "Can we climb in there with you?"

"Don't you wish you had a tent now, big man?" Alissa smirked. "I guess you can come in, but I'll put it on your tab."

Rain fell heavily, drenching them as they began to sardine themselves into a tent not made to accommodate five. They were forced to sit on top of each other while listening to the downpour just beyond the thin layer of canvas at their backs. Lightning flashed and its brilliance lit the forest with white-blue light. The thunder shook the insides of those trapped in such close quarters. Wes unzipped the door, his disappointment apparent as he yanked the zipper closed once more.

"Our supplies. The fuckin' packs are out there!"

"What are we going to do?" Kelly asked.

Dennis held up the only thing he managed to salvage before retreating into the tent, the whiskey bottle.

"We're gonna ride this bitch out and find the Professor tomorrow!"

****

A storm rose quickly on the horizon. Lightning danced erratically above the canopy of the trees. The dark sky spilled rain violently down upon the professor's meager camp, battering his tent. He regretted not staying hidden within the caves where he would have stayed dry. Tree branches reached down to claw at the canvas of his only sanctuary, leaving him hoping the tent would prove to be as leak-proof as advertised. He heaved a sigh of relief, remembering he left most of his equipment at the bottom of the cavern entrance or it would have gotten wet.

He held the disc in his dirt-caked hands. It was heavy for its size, which was about ten inches in diameter. Professor Lipton used his own spit and forefinger to remove centuries of dust, which was not exactly the proper method, yet his excitement got the better of him. The disc was carved with markings similar to those he had read about before, however those were uncovered in temples in Mexico. He laid the artifact in his lap, shaking his head.

"Why can't they just accept this or at least broaden their minds to the possibility," he thought. He pictured his colleagues on the scientific board. They were those men and women who didn't believe the history books should be rewritten to add a chapter about a scattering civilization or how a handful of them had found refuge in present day Georgia. Dr. Lipton, unlike those same men and women, had been in the field most of his career, witnessing first hand things that most would consider unbelievable. He had the face of any man in their sixties, yet his eyes held the wanderlust of someone much younger. Nothing could kill his thirst for knowledge...not even cancer. The board was a council of naysayers, yet there he sat, staring down at a truth that would silence them once and for all.

Dr. Lipton wrapped the artifact in a scrap of cloth, and then zipped it up in his pack. He brushed the dirt and leaves from his sleeping bag, cursing himself for not taking his boots off before climbing in. The wind whipped and whistled around his two-man tent. The silhouette of rain wound its way down all sides; its shadow looked like liquid serpents. His stomach was empty so he attempted to satisfy it with a zip lock bag of trail mix. He couldn't leave, it was not an option. He just hoped Wes would be able to locate him. His present camp was off course from the map he provided the young man. He planned on hiking out in an attempt to meet up with his associate professor beside the stream in which he intended to camp, and then lead him and his companions back to assist in further studies. He thought the note he had left his administrator may have seemed cryptic, yet his whereabouts had to remain secret until he was certain of what he suspected to be true. Wes would be the only person to know he was actually on a completely different mountain than he proclaimed to be excavating.

Amidst the storm there came a rhythmic thump. A drum? At first he guessed it to be the thunderheads above him until it seemed to slow down, matching the pace of his stammering heart. He scrambled from his tent, shielding his face as he trudged out into the rain. He approached the source of the drumming. He stood at the edge of the entryway to the cavern, and his eyes were met by utter darkness, yet the thrumming continued. He stood motionless, his mind trying to grasp if it was reality or only an act of nature fooling him. He fell back as the blast of a conch shell came shaking from his insides. He pushed himself to his feet, and as the rain fell continuously, he was forced to wipe his eyes with the sleeve of his flannel shirt. He took three cautious steps to stare into the hole once more. Disbelief flooded him as he reached forward, his hands feeling for the rope he had in place so that he could climb in and out of the hidden chamber. His curiosity over-ruled a sinking feeling in his gut and the nagging told him he needed to grab his helmet. He fitted himself hastily with his climbing harness, and then gripping the line, he began lowering himself into the total darkness, knowing at the bottom he had left a lantern.

He began to ease into his descent when he felt something give way beneath his weight. The harness was breaking. His rain-slick hands lost their purchase of the rope and in a panic he tightened his grip only to feel his palms burning and blistering. In seconds, he met the stone floor of the chamber below, his shin bones shattered in a violent instant causing them to protrude through his skin. His body went into immediate shock, leaving him gasping for air. Once his lungs were full, he cried out until his throat was raw. He turned to his side to empty the trail mix from his convulsing stomach. He heard nothing over his labored breathing. The shadows wavered as if he were not alone. Movement before him caught what little attention he could muster over the severity of his injuries. It seemed as though there was a mass of darkness before him which wasdense, black, and undulating only feet away. He could hear the faint tinkling of bells. Before his eyes, a vision materialized of a muscular man wearing a headdress of elaborate feathers. His body was painted red and white and his face paint depicted a skull. He wore an obsidian necklace around his neck. The entity was covered in the skin of a jaguar as a loin cloth and in his hand he held a stone vessel. He dipped his long fingers within it, began speaking a dead language, and then he anointed the professor's face. Dr. Lipton's legs were in absolute agony, but when he realized what the shaman had decorated him with, his body went numb. He had painted him Mayan Blue, the pigment used to symbolize the sacrifice of flesh and blood. The professor's heart stuttered when the spectral man grinned, his toned body disintegrating into a corpse, his face peeling away, sloughing off to the cavern floor. The painted skull was gone to reveal the yellowed bone beneath. Bells hung in its tangled dry hair. Thunder boomed from the black sky and lightening flashed down from the opening above. In a momentary flash, the visage of bone took on the appearance of an owl with golden eyes. Professor Lipton's consciousness left him.

****

Professor Lipton awoke to find the adrenaline in his body was spent. The excruciating pain couldn't be held at bay. Above him moved a shadow, and startled, he fought to flee. His arms had grown numb. His spine ached with each movement as he tried to free himself. It was then he realized he was no longer at the bottom of the cave entrance, but was bound backwards over a jagged stone somewhere deep within the hidden chambers of the mountain. A faint blue light revealed the specter materializing once more. In his terror, he recognized it from studying the hieroglyphics recording its presence amongst the now-dead civilization of the Mayans. The entity was Ah-Puch, the Lord of Death, controller of Xibalba (or the land of fear, which was the Mayan equivalent of the underworld). The massive chamber permeated the stench of decay and blood and it crawled down his throat, eliciting a wave of extreme nausea. The shadows writhed about him as a hundred sets of eyes opened, casting an unearthly golden light and illuminating the Lord of Death. Beyond them came monstrous cries, and howling of hungry creatures. His captor's body was of a bloated corpse; his head was of an owl and it twitched side-to-side in a movement akin to the natural form of the bird. About his throat hung the legendary adornment of disembodied eyes hanging from nerve cords, his symbolic marker. He lifted a decay-blackened hand which held an obsidian knife, sharp and jagged. The voice of Ah-Puch resonated off the stone walls deep and hollow as it spoke the words of the ancient priests.

Again came morbid cheering, though Dr. Lipton could not see from whom they came.

"NO! PLEASE!" the professor begged.

The dagger of black stone was brought down into his chest and fiery pain erupted around the cold blade. He could feel his ribs and sternum being roughly shattered in the cruel motions of the stone knife. His blood poured fast and hot from the wound as the Lord of Death worked it wider. His screams were choked in his throat as his mouth filled with bile and blood. His chest became an open cavity as it was wrenched apart, and the musty cavern air filled the gaping hole. In a swift motion setting the professor's nerves on fire, Ah- Puch tore Dr. Lipton's heart free and held it aloft. It beat feebly in his palm for a moment. He placed it upon a stone and went back to his work, digging the dagger into the professor's abdomen. The shadows fell upon the heart, picking it to pieces and as they fed they began to take shape. He cut through the blue- painted skin before running his hands down into what was once Professor Lipton's stomach. The golden eyes watching over the sacrifice moved in unison, and then burst into a cloud of screeching beaks and feathers. The cluster of owls taking flight weren't at all natural, but a legion of aviary specters all commanded by the underworld god who now gripped fistfuls of the professor's innards. He danced wildly, stirring the ghost birds into a frenzy before they went screeching from the cave, leaving only death and darkness behind them. The Lord of Death leaned over the dead man's face to retrieve the last of his grizzly trophies, and then the blue eyes of the professor were hung among the rest about his neck.

****

Those who imbibed too much the night before awoke to the shock of the sun's bright rays. Wes and Alissa were the only ones ready to break camp to continue at the predetermined time. Wes busied himself with salvaging what he could from their wet backpacks. Luckily only a few things were lost, though one particular item concerned Tyler greatly.

"The ass wipe got soaked!"

"Leaves?" Dennis teased.

"Get up princess!"

Alissa kicked the side of the tent and Kelly moaned. It took her another half an hour to emerge from its zipped up door, forcing sunglasses over her eyes in exasperation.

"What fucking time is it?" Kelly complained.

"Too damn early," Tyler agreed as he sipped a bottle of water.

Alissa downed their tent before forcing it into her damp pack, sighing as her dormmate whined continuously about the dirt on her new tennis shoes, the sunburn on her shoulder blades, and the bug bites she suffered the night before.

"Let's get moving," Wes interrupted, suffering a sidelong glance from Kelly who just started to search for something for breakfast.

"This isn't the Holiday Inn, so grab something that you can eat as we walk."

Alissa finally rummaged through the zippered pouch of her pack and tossed a cereal bar at the blonde who huffed like a child.

"The terrain gets a little rougher from here," Wes spoke as they set out. "This is where you start earning your extra credit."

He was wearing a worn-out shirt. Alissa could tell his body was toned, not overly muscular, but definitely up to the task of the long hike he had scheduled for them; it was a new side of him, it only made her want him more. She fell in line right behind him, determined to show him she could keep up with him physically as well as mentally.

****

They stopped next to a small stream meandering through the hills to eat a light lunch. Kelly slipped off her shoes to let the cool water trickle over her feet. Tyler took the opportunity to sit behind her to massage her shoulders.

"Easy on the sunburn," Kelly complained before turning her attention to Wes. "How far do we have to go?"

"As the crow flies, about two more miles," he estimated.

"What do you mean, as the crow flies?" she sighed then wiped the sweat from her face.

35

"We're leaving the trail behind us, can you handle that?" Wes asked.

"You'll be alright. I can carry you if you want?" Dennis offered causing Alissa to nearly vomit on his feet. Kelly was satisfied by his generosity and began drying her feet to pull her shoes back on.

****

Wes took the lead once more as the others trailed behind him. It wasn't long before Kelly threatened to stop.

"I can't do this shit!"

"We can't stop now, get moving." Wes said.

"I just said...I... CAN'T! "

"We don't have a choice." Alissa spoke. "We have been hiking for nearly two days and we aren't going back now."

Alissa was spent, her body ached, and now her concentration was broken by her dormmate's refusal to keep going.

"Can't we rest for a while? Is it really going to matter if we're an hour off schedule?" The blonde sat upon a large rock, then rummaged through her pack.

"I need a drink and an hour to catch my breath or I'm taking Dennis up on his offer to carry me."

"Come on, Kelly!" Alissa shook her head.

The longer Alissa stood still the more her determination waned.

"I'll give you fifteen minutes then we will go or you can sit your ass on that rock and wait until we get back!" Wes stated.

He felt no need to coddle her, nor was he afraid of the cavemen presently competing for her attention. This was his expedition and he wouldn't tolerate any bullshit.

"That could take days!"

Wes didn't answer as he took a seat not far away on a tree stump, then pulled out his map to study their progress. His bold behavior made Alissa smile.

CHAPTER TWO

The Owl wheeled above, staring down at them as a brief argument erupted. Its feathers fluttered in the breezes of approaching autumn. It descended to perch upon the lowest branches of an oak tree, peering through its golden orbs, keeping vigilant watch of those approaching its home. Its head spun nearly in a full circle as it eyed the girl with blonde hair sitting beneath it.

"WHAT.THE.FUCK!"

Kelly leaped from her seat raging, causing the group to jump, and after a moment of realization they broke into winded laughter. She wiped a hefty helping of bird shit from her shoulder.

"You got what you deserve, cry baby!" Alissa giggled.

Even Wes laughed heartily as Kelly held her hand out in front of her, dripping green bird droppings and gagging.

"I'll help, Kell," Tyler offered.

He opened his water bottle to dowse her hand clean. She stripped off the tank top she wore and attempted to wipe any remnants from the side of her neck before tossing it over the mountain side they steadily climbed all day.

"I need a god damn shower!" Kelly's voice shook with anger, bringing tears to her eyes.

"Our camp is near a stream if you'd hurry your ass up. We're burning daylight!" Wes informed her, his face was red with amusement.

Kelly nodded her head as her determination returned. She cursed the owl that left her stinking even more than the tedious hike. The hooting above her seemed to mock her frustration as the bird took flight with a beating of its great wings.

"Come down here, you bastard! I'll show you to shit on me!" she raged before flinging a rock at her offender.

****

They steadily kept climbing, and after a distance, the terrain leveled out. The breeze was cool, but the company dripped sweat. The thoughts of stopping to camp became the reward keeping their exhausted bodies moving. Alissa fought to stay close to Wes. The elevation change clenched her chest, but she wanted to prove she could handle the journey. She found her thighs ached from scaling rocks and fallen trees. Perspiration dripped from her underarms and she knew her shirt must be drenched. Embarrassment flooded her. Her brother used to call his excessive sweating "swamp pits," and she nearly laughed at the thoughts of how unflattering she must look. Alissa noticed then that Wes too sported some gnarly pit stains and her self-consciousness began to diminish.

"Why didn't we go to Brasstown? I thought that was where the settlement was?" Alissa asked, trying to keep her voice strong and not completely winded.

"The professor discovered what he believes to be a map to an undiscovered settlement here on Blood Mountain," Wes answered.

"Who the hell named it that?" Tyler asked. "Sounds like some devil worshipper shit."

"The Cherokee, actually," Wes answered. "Near the summit, reddish-colored lichen and Catawba grows. Some say it's actually stained from all the blood that was shed in a horrendous battle between the Cherokee and the Cree Indians."

"I thought it was named that after a missing hiker girl was found murdered up here," Tyler said.

"Don't try to scare us!" Kelly dismissed his attempt at creeping them out.

Conversation died, and all that could be heard was the heavy breathing from a day spent hiking up the mountain side. The hoot of an owl incited another round of out- of-breath laughter from all but Kelly, who cursed the bird again.

"We will be pitching a camp soon, which should make Kelly happy!" Wes announced.

"Sure as hell does," she said.

****

The campfire crackled then spit embers into the failing light.

"Point me in the direction of that stream. I need to get this sweat and bird shit off of me!" Kelly said, opening her pack to search for clean clothes.

"It's down the hill a bit, you can't miss it."

Kelly shoved her clothes beneath her arm, along with a flashlight, before taking off in the direction of her much-needed bath.

"I think I'll accompany her," Tyler winked, then trotted off behind the fit blonde who was clothed only in shorts and a sports bra.

"COCK BLOCKER!" Dennis yelled as he took a seat beside Alissa and Wes.

"What kind of discovery did Professor Lipton make?" Alissa asked.

"A map to something important inside of a cave," Wes grinned. "He set it up for us to meet him out here and assist him in bringing it back."

"Do you think he found what he was looking for?"

"I believe so, and even though all of these people think he has lost his mind, I have faith in him. I think once this week is over he'll be hailed as an archaeological hero," Wes spoke.

Alissa could hear the confidence in his reply and his excitement radiated from him.

"And we will be there right along with him," Dennis grinned. "Oprah, here we come!"

An owl hooted in the distance making them laugh as Dennis's eyes strayed in the direction of where Kelly and Tyler went. Alissa could see a hint of jealousy in his face when she looked across their small fire and it caused a guilty sense of satisfaction to rise in her belly.

****

Kelly stripped down on the bank before stepping into the cool water, splashing it over her skin. It took her breath away as she waded out into its chilly depths before kneeling down to submerge as much of her body as she could. The air held a snap to it, signaling the beginning of autumn. It left her feeling a little cold, but Kelly was determined to return to camp refreshed and clean.

"Boo!" Tyler hollered causing Kelly to nearly topple over on the slick rocks along the creek bottom.

"You bastard!" she giggled as she cupped her hands over her breasts.

"There's no need to hide," he said. "Do you mind if I join you?" Tyler asked.

"Not at all," Kelly smiled.

He dipped his toe on the edge of the water, and then jumped back.

"How the hell can you stand being in there? It's freezing!"

"Scared of shrinkage?" Kelly asked before bursting out into laughter.

"Come out of that water and I'll show you shrinkage!" he said pointing down to his crotch.

Tyler shook his head as he spied her clothes folded neatly on a flat rock.

"I'll show you to be a smart ass!"

Tyler swept up her only clothing, then stepped back from the stream, pretending he would leave her there naked and cold. Kelly stood, still attempting to cover herself, then splashed through the water. She stepped onto the bank shivering and bare from the waist down. Kelly could see he had no intentions of leaving her there so she dropped her hands, giving him the full view.

"Can I have my clothes back? Please?" Her voice sent a rush up Tyler's spine.

"Come get them."

Kelly knew he was going to kiss her, run his hands down her body, and let his fingers glide softly over her skin.

She was keeping a mental tally going between him and his best friend; Tyler would soon be on top in more ways than one. Kelly could feel herself wanting to strip off his clothes and feel more than his chest against her. She stepped closer to him, and then ran her hands up his chest. His muscles beneath his shirt sent a thrill up her spine. Kelly leaned against him, letting him feel her wet body against his through his thin layer of clothing. He bent down and kissed her, sliding his hands down the smooth skin of her naked back, and stopped to grab her bare ass. She could feel him getting aroused as her hand explored the bulge in his shorts. A stench seemed to invade both of their noses at once.

"My god, Tyler, what is that?" Kelly asked, nearly gagging.

"I'm not sure," he answered.

He didn't want to stop what they started, but Kelly was now really concerned as a second wave of the vile stench drifted to them again.

Tyler reluctantly handed her the dry clothes he teasingly stole.

"I have heard that bears smell, maybe it's a brown bear."

She rushed to dress herself, though her clothes clung to areas of her body that weren't dry enough, causing her to panic.

He put his arm around Kelly once she was clothed, then they hurried back in the direction of camp. He only hoped for being her hero she would reward him by continuing with their tryst back at camp.

****

The bird sat perched on a limb above its companion's head, and awaited any commands. The moonlight overhead shimmered hauntingly down upon what was once Professor Lipton. He stood hunkered over, standing upon broken and twisted legs. The compound fractures in both of his shins sent his bones protruding through his mottled skin. Those shards were forced back into his blue-stained flesh before being tied off with strips of leather. Black blood clung half-coagulated to his lower legs and down to his feet as remnants of what fell from the gaping holes in his abdomen and chest. He was a walking corpse controlled by the will of

Ah-Puch. The reek hanging about him was so intolerable and putrid it sent the two he was watching fleeing back to the safety of their firelight. Dr. Lipton placed a blistered and weeping palm against the bark of the tree as he tilted his head; listening to the voices of the humans at the top of the hill as they talked. He took a shambling step towards the creek bed, then smelled the air, which was rich with smoke. He slowly began making his way toward it.

****

"By tomorrow, we should be meeting up with the professor, so we should all get some rest," Wes said and stretched, then went to work unrolling his sleeping bag.

Alissa and Kelly climbed inside the cramped tent.

"You smell! Why didn't you take a bath?" Kelly asked.

"Fuck off, princess!" Alissa yawned as she felt her body resigning itself to the arms of sleep.

"I'm kinda freaked out," Kelly whispered.

"If there is a bear out there it will eat the guys first so don't worry," Alissa answered, teasing Kelly about the animal they claimed they smelled by the stream.

Kelly laughed softly before pulling her sleeping bag up around her ears. Alissa was often annoyed by her dormmate, but she found she genuinely liked the stereotypical college girl beside her.

"I'm slightly disappointed," Kelly spoke softly.

"Why?" Alissa asked, knowing by the tone of her voice Kelly was going to say something naughty.

"Tyler was going to show it to me, but we got interrupted," Kelly giggled. "It's big. I felt it through his shorts!"

"Shut up and go to sleep, pervert!" Alissa laughed.

"Don't be a prude! I know you want to bang Wes."

Alissa forced her hand over Kelly's mouth. "SHHHHHH!"

Kelly pulled Alissa's hand away before putting her lips close to her friend's ear. "You're hot for teacher!" she teased.

"Enough! Go to bed!" Alissa ordered.

In the dark she felt her face burning with embarrassment, but she knew it was true.

****

The fire died to a pile of glowing embers. The three young men were rolled up in their sleeping bags breathing softly. The abomination housed within the flesh and bone suit of Professor Lipton stood beyond the edge of the campsite. It lurched forward before cocking its head to the side. It stood only feet from Tyler's head. The owl came fluttering from the trees to land upon its shoulder. The depths of the earth called out to the undead slave that was once the elderly professor, and the Lord of Death bid him return to his subterranean home. The trap would soon be set to lure the humans into those dark chambers. The owl took flight as the walking corpse backed away into the darkness of the forest, leaving only its stench behind. The bird sat upon the limb of a dead tree, its incessant calling shattered the silent serenity of the camp below. The sleeping bags began to wiggle and writhe as the young men awoke.

"What the fuck?" Dennis's voice was groggy with sleep.

The hoot persisted in an almost mocking tone. A flashlight flipped on, casting a white orb against the side of the tent. Silhouettes of the two girls danced inside as they were awakened.

"You've got to be fuckin' kidding me!" Alissa said, and then pulled her pack over her face to shield her eyes from the sudden intrusion of light.

"How can I sleep with this shit? I hiked all damn day, got crapped on, and now THIS!" Kelly bitched.

Kelly fought with the zipper before yanking the canvas door open. Her hand fumbled in the dirt to locate a fist-sized rock which she used as a projectile, but missed the owl. It took flight and left a single feather drifting down to her. She picked it up, and then crumpled it in her palm.

Kelly's nose caught the scent of something so foul it sent her ducking back into the tent.

"WAKE UP! That smell is back!" Kelly hollered.

"We're awake," Wes said softly.

He scanned the shadows of the trees. "We will have to be certain there isn't a bear."

"I'm killing that feathered asshole if I get a chance," Dennis said.

CHAPTER THREE

Sunrise came far too early for the group since they hadn't gotten any real sleep. They never found any sign of a large predator, but every time they seemed to get settled in, the hoot of an owl came to haunt them from their slumber. Twice Tyler went out into the darkness to silence the winged nuisance only to be eluded.

Breakfast was only granola bars and bottled water around a dead fire. They set out in silence on the last leg of the hike in search of the professor who was supposed to be waiting for them. The forest smelled like fall and the peaceful trickling of the stream nearby made Alissa wish she could stop and rest upon its bank. The weather was pleasant among the trees, and soon they would begin their autumnal metamorphosis. If it wasn't for the forced march it would have been a marvelous experience.

"I'm so damn tired," Kelly broke the silence.

"It will only be a few hours and we will reach the rendezvous point," Wes assured not only her, but the rest of the group.

He halted to look down at the marker on his folded-up map, then squinted at his compass.

"Just think, Kell, after we meet up with Indiana Lipton and carry back this artifact he thinks he has found, we're gonna be famous!"

"I hope you're right." She smiled over at Dennis.

The air was clean, it held no aroma of any wild animals, and the strange events of the night before drifted to the backs of their minds. As noon neared, they finally reached their destination. Much to their relief the meeting spot was next to the creek. The water trickled serenely, banishing the exhaustion from their bones. The girls decided to brave the chilly water and waded out into it, exploring the rocky banks. The water gathered, then flowed over the top of a small waterfall no taller than Alissa, who was enchanted by the scenery.

"I'm going to dig out my cell to get a few pictures," Alissa said.

"Oh yes, we do need a group picture. I have something better than a cell phone." Dennis opened his backpack and pulled out a lightweight camera.

"We can use the digital camera, and it has plenty of space for a few pics of our faithful group."

They stood together on the dark bank of the stream watching the tiny, red light flashing on the camera positioned on a rock not far away. They squeezed together and smiled. The camera went off, but in the same instant Tyler jumped back and began a tirade of cuss words crude enough to make a trucker blush. A slimy white and green trail ran down his right cheek. There was a split second of his rage building before the familiar call of the owl sent him into a violent eruption. He began scooping up rocks from the creek bed, and then pelting the bird as it retreated to the highest branches of an Ash tree.

"Son of a bitch!"

Tyler stumbled through the creek, nearly falling on his face. He chased after the bird as it took off through the trees.

"Tyler!" Alissa called after him, but he wouldn't return. He could be seen zig-zagging through the thick brush and lichen-blanketed trees.

"Let's go get him," Dennis motioned to Wes.

"You ladies wait here for Professor Lipton," he instructed as he followed behind Dennis.

****

They followed in the direction in which they could hear Tyler's voice still cursing the owl.

"Get back here!" Dennis yelled. "We don't have time for this shit!"

Wes glanced at his watch, and then shook his head. "This is ridiculous."

He was already worried that the professor wasn't there to meet them, now this situation with Tyler only increased his anxiety.

"Where the hell did he go?" Dennis asked.

It seemed as though Tyler was swallowed up by the forest. The woods were completely silent now, not even the owl could be heard. They continued in the direction in which he was last spotted barreling through the bushes, but the farther they went, the seemingly simple task began twisting into an unbelievable mystery.

****

"What an idiot!" Kelly said.

They took a seat on the creek bed to eat freeze-dried meals for lunch.

"I'm going to starve to death!" Alissa laughed.

Their packs held enough food to last a week, but it was a collection of meager meals, plus a few snacks.

"It's a good diet, I guess," Kelly said, spooning food into her mouth.

"I need a cappuccino though; this no-coffee deal is hell!"

"I think Tyler had some in his pack," Alissa offered.

"That's not coffee, that's shit water!" Kelly wrinkled her nose.

They paused in their conversation to listen for any sign of Tyler being brought back.

"At least we get a break," Kelly smiled.

Though lunch was far from satisfying, the chance to sit down and breathe definitely was.

They rested as the lazy sounds of the trickling stream passed along with the hours.

****

"It all looks the same out here," Dennis said and his observation sent a sudden chill through Wes.

"We need to find him and get back on-track," Wes responded, glancing once more at his watch.

The hours passed without a sign of Tyler, a gnawing at Wes's gut told him something was very wrong.

"Maybe we should go back and get the girls. I mean, what if we get separated?"

"I know the way back," Wes answered, but the second his response passed his lips a wave of doubt washed over him.

Dennis looked him in the eye, and then shook his head. "Are you sure, man?"

Before Wes could answer, a scream tore through the forest.

****

"Where are they?" Alissa thought out loud.

"Where is the professor? Shouldn't he be here?" Kelly asked.

"Maybe we're all lost Are you sure Wes was following the directions correctly?" the blonde added before standing up to look in all directions.

"Don't say that!" Alissa's voice shook.

"They'll be back soon," she added, in an attempt to remain calm.

Alissa glanced at her watch, and it was now nearly 3 p.m. They should have met up with the professor hours before. Her heart sank. She went to her pack, then began riffling through it. They all knew there would be no cell phone reception, so they placed all their phones in a waterproof storage bag and agreed Alissa would carry them. She removed handfuls of clothing and other gear to locate the small bag.

Alissa turned them on one-by-one and her assumption was crushingly correct: not a one had service. Defeated, she put them back in her pack, then turned to see Kelly pacing the edge of the creek.

"Listen, Wes left his pack. It has the map, and if shit gets out of control, we will follow it back to the van and drive out for help," Alissa said.

Kelly stood for a moment, thinking before finally smiling weakly and nodding.

"Yeah, we can do that."

****

Wes and Dennis rushed forward, listening as the screams continued. They were filled with anguish; the cries of a man in tremendous pain.

"Over there!"

Dennis sprinted ahead of Wes who from the corner of his eyes caught a break in the bushes, then the dropping of the hillside. He caught Dennis by the collar of his shirt and yanked him back before he went leaping over the rhododendron, then tumbling over the edge. They fell back upon the dirt, and when the screams began again, they knew they located Tyler. Wes crawled forward to look down the steep incline. Tyler lay on his back, holding his right arm against his chest. The drop met a long slope riddled with jagged rocks that protruded like broken teeth.

"You fuckin' idiot...you chased an owl right off the edge!" Dennis yelled.

"I had that little fucker!"

Tyler held a handful of feathers in his good hand.

"Please, God, HELP ME!" Tyler's next pleas came with saddening urgency.

It was obvious from their vantage point he must have tumbled over the hillside in pursuit of the bird and went rolling down it. Tyler must have been so close to succeeding when the earth literally disappeared from beneath his feet.

"We can hike down on the eastern side," Wes said and pointed out a safe route to retrieve Tyler.

"It has some places that we can make it down to him."

"How badly are you hurt?" Wes asked.

"My arm, I know it's broken, but I think the rest of me is ok, just hurry up," Tyler said, his face pale.

They made their way slowly around before coming to a spot accommodating enough to attempt a rescue. Wes went first, and with each step he tested the earth beneath his foot to make sure it wouldn't give away. Dennis came along behind him as they inched their way towards Tyler.

Each time Tyler cried out, it sent a sense of agonizing urgency through them.

"HURRY UP, PLEASE!!"

"WE'RE COMIN BRO!" Dennis reassured him.

Wes scanned their surroundings, and then spotted something. A tent at the bottom of the hill.

****

The two young women sat nervously waiting as the sun began to set.

"If they don't come back..."

"Don't say that." Kelly said, tears threatened to fall.

"If they don't come back, we head out in the morning," Alissa repeated. "We should build a fire soon and set up our tent"

"What if they were attacked by a bear?" Kelly asked.

"Don't think like that."

Alissa was trying to keep her mind focused as the thoughts of a hungry bear threatened to shake her resolve. The hoot of an owl drove a stake through the heart of her bravery.

"SHUT UP, ASSHOLE!"

A voice yelled and she nearly burst into tears. Through the tree line, Alissa could see the two young men making their way quickly back to the creek.

"OVER HERE!" Alissa screamed, then began waving her arms.

"Thank God! Where's Tyler?" Kelly asked, before wading through the creek to greet them.

"He broke his arm. We left him in a safe spot just long enough to come get you," Dennis said.

"Grab the packs, we found the professor's camp," Wes instructed.

"Well, Tyler found it!" Dennis teased.

****

The sun was going down, and the horizon bled as it sunk low and they stood at the edge of the hillside.

"Flashlights," said Wes, and their beams lit the steep pathway.

"Why didn't he meet us?" asked Alissa.

"That's what we're gonna find out. If the tent is his it's off course, so I suspect he came across something very important," Wes answered.

Wes stepped down softly, and as he did he carefully placed his foot and tested the stability of the earth beneath it. He used his hands to steady himself before looking back, nodding to the others. Alissa and Kelly came next with Dennis bringing up the rear and keeping close to Kelly to ensure she didn't tumble down and take those in front of her down with her.

The descent was so time-consuming they did not reach flat ground until the moon climbed into the sky above them. The flashlight beams bounced ahead of them as they made their way to the yellow canvas tent in the distance.

Alissa could see Tyler's silhouette sitting in front of it, his arm cradled against his chest.

"I hope Professor Lipton is ok," Alissa said as they approached the dark camp.

CHAPTER FOUR

It could hear their voices, smell the blood of Tyler's wounds.

****

The tent was empty, but for Dr. Lipton's belongings. Wes pulled the professor's pack out, then sat upon a fallen tree. It felt heavy in his hands as he unzipped it. His hands shook when his eyes came across the disc-shaped object wrapped in cloth. He directed Alissa to hold her flashlight directly over it as he carefully removed the artifact from its wrapping.

"I knew it!"

"What is it?" Alissa asked.

"I'll have to examine it further, but I can see that it bears the same markings as the tablet recovered at the other sites."

"What are they? The markings?"

"Constellations.They tell of a great tragedy and they are the same that were discovered on stones in Mexico."

Wes smiled up at her and she knew the professor had found something extraordinary.

"I'll make a fire," Dennis said.

Kelly helped Tyler to rest comfortably atop his unrolled sleeping bag inside of the professor's tent.

"Let's sit over there. I'll be able to get a better look."

Wes grinned before gently carrying the disc closer to the campfire.

The campfire blazed and popped as Dennis fed it dry wood. Kelly sat attending Tyler who was in severe pain. She handed him a handful of prescription pain medication.

"I tore ligaments in my knee last year playing tennis, and these should make the pain more bearable," Kelly told him.

Alissa sat beside of Wes as he inspected the disc. Its edges were fairly jagged and he ran his finger over it as he thought for a moment.

"This is only a piece of something amazing," he said.

"There's more?" Alissa asked.

"I believe so, and it appears to be some sort of seal. There must be a doorway close by."

"Maybe he is still working wherever he discovered this," Alissa said.

"I would almost guarantee it. He never gives up!" Wes smiled.

"I suspect this to be a part of a door, possibly a burial chamber." His eyes met hers as he continued.

"If he uncovered the remains of Mayans, here in Georgia, it would change history books!"

Alissa leaned closer to him, feigning the depths of her interest only to feel his skin brush against her arm. "Amazing!"

It made sense to her now why the cavemen were enlisted to help, as a stone doorway would definitely take muscle to move. Alissa began to think Dennis's dreams of being on Oprah weren't so far-fetched.

Wes held the disc closer to his face, rubbing dirt away with his fingertip.

"MAYAN BLUE!"

"The paint that they used, am I right?" Alissa asked, recalling all she could from her history classes.

"Yes, more proof."

"How are you feeling?" Kelly asked Tyler as she caressed his cheek.

"It hurts like hell, but I'll live. Thanks for the meds, I think they'll help," he answered.

"After we find the professor tomorrow, we will hike you out of here," Wes offered.

70

"Sounds like a plan," Tyler agreed thankfully.

****

The moon was a silver disc casting its light down upon the small camp in the middle of the rolling forests. Wes hadn't stopped gazing at the artifact long enough to even eat dinner.

"They used Mayan Blue to paint temples, pottery, murals... and also, on those marked for ritual sacrifice." He educated Alissa further as the night wore on.

"It's incredibly weather-resistant. Can you imagine how old this is?"

"You sure know a lot about that stuff," Kelly said, and yawned. "I'm turning in for the night."

"Professor Lipton is my idol; I saw him speak when I was in fifth grade and instantly knew I had to become an archaeologist," Wes said.

Kelly went climbing into Alissa's tent without another word. She was completely exhausted and couldn't muster a polite response. Her body ached as she started to

71

wish she had never tagged along. At that moment Kelly could've been in her dorm getting ready for the night, probably to go to dinner with the girls and dancing in the club, and most definitely, a long hot shower. Tyler and Dennis both were very promising prospects as far as her plan to marry a go-getter, but her affection for them waned tremendously each moment she spent in the middle of the forest with them. The only silver lining was the possibility of becoming famous when the old professor revealed his great secret to the world. Maybe Kelly would get lucky and score a role in a reality TV show. She fell asleep thinking about those kinds of fanciful possibilities, because they were the only things keeping her from having a nervous breakdown.

****

"She just isn't made for this type of thing," Alissa said and Wes nodded.

"She really wasn't supposed to come, but she invited herself when she heard Tyler and Dennis talking about it. I guess she figured it would just be a party weekend."

"Well, I hate to disappoint her," Wes answered, his voice was thick with sarcasm.

"Tell us more about that thing, professor," Dennis said, as he stuffed his mouth full of potato chips. He shook the bag in frustration realizing most of them were ground to dust by the weight of the gear in his pack.

"Not a full-fledged professor quite yet, not with the experience of Dr. Lipton, but I can decipher its meaning," Wes said.

"I can tell you that all the signs point to this disc being of Mayan origin, and since the edges are jagged, I would say it's only part of something larger," Wes answered.

"The hieroglyphics are reminiscent of those found in Mexico and tell of the destruction of their society. It wouldn't be here if they hadn't migrated this way."

"That's some crazy shit, man!" Dennis answered.

"There's also mention of bloodletting or suicide in order to stop whatever plagued them."

"Suicide?" Alissa asked.

"Yes, it was considered quite honorable. The spilling of one's own blood was a great deed back then, as the goddess Ixtab would carry a soul away to paradise for committing suicide. In this case, it was an escape from Hell."

"I'd hate to see their version of Hell if dudes that committed suicide went to heaven," Dennis said.

"It was a place of fear and death. The lord that ruled over it had complete power over the spirits within his realm, causing them terror and pain long after their hearts stopped beating."

"Even after they were dead?" Alissa asked.

"Yes." Wes looked to her, his eyes fixed upon her.

"He could recall their spirits back into their corpses to kill them over and over again...not even death was a release." He burst out laughing, causing Alissa to slap his arm.

"You're trying to scare me!" she said.

"What's a campfire without a good scary story?" he teased.

"Chill out, Alissa. Kelly's the only drama queen we need around camp," Dennis laughed.

****

They all retired for the night. The two women shared their tent while Wes helped Tyler into Professor Lipton's. He climbed in behind him, then motioned to Dennis.

"I'll sleep out here. That tent's a sausage party!" teased Dennis.

"Suit yourself," Wes yawned.

****

The fire dwindled to a faint glow as the group slept off the heavy slumber brought on by physical exertion, and in Tyler's case, a cocktail of far too much prescription pain medication and bodily trauma that left him completely unconscious and unaware of what was taking place in the darkness beyond the canvas tent. Dennis was lying on his back, his face to the stars. His snores were loud. They would've been intrusive if the others hadn't been so exhausted.

****

The cavern was an unearthly black hole not far from the camp. If they hadn't been so worn out, the humans may have discovered it, and then found the rope leading into its depths. Those fluttering and climbing along the cold stone walls didn't need the tattered rope to ascend from the caverns for they bore wings with misshapen hands on their tips, clawed feet, and abnormally large heads. They had golden eyes, and their appearance was meant to be some twisted rendition of an owl. They completed their transformation before swarming from the open maw of the cave. They fluttered, and then hopped about the dead fire to perch around those sleeping deeply. Their heads twitched from side-to-side. In unison, the Wayob began their assault on the silence about them.

HOO-HOO...HOO-HOO...HOO-HOO...

****

The sudden onslaught of sound shook Dennis from his sleep. His eyes opened in confusion and disbelief. He sat forward before nearly screaming at the sight of the shadows surrounding him. Fear held him there unable to move, his terror seized his chest tightly. He dared not even breathe. The intruder's eyes shown golden yellow beneath the moon and their silhouettes struck recognition within his brain. His breath eased out of his chest at knowing it was only birds, but his skin rose in gooseflesh at the sheer numbers of them. Dennis had never seen such a mass of owls and he couldn't recall them traveling in flocks like other birds. He wondered then if it weren't breeding season or if there was some other natural explanation for their presence.

Dennis slowly eased the zipper down on his sleeping bag. He felt trapped inside it, unable to run if he felt the need. Dennis cursed himself for not sleeping in the tent with Wes and Tyler. He knew they were only birds, yet he was still unnerved by them. Dennis slipped out of the bag, then began crawling towards the tents on the other side of the fire. The birds continued in their raucous behavior, seemingly becoming more agitated by his retreat. They hooted and screeched, eyeing him suspiciously. He was halfway to his destination when Kelly broke his concentration by cussing and rummaging through her pack. She turned on her flashlight, and it flooded the dark surroundings causing the birds to burst into flight.

"What is that?" Kelly asked.

"Owls," he whispered, but she couldn't hear him over the din of the birds screeching and their wings flapping.

"Wake up, Alissa!" Kelly urged.

Dennis could see her shadow on the side of the tent as she shook the other girl awake.

"There's something outside."

"What...?" Alissa finally awoke.

"Don't you hear that?"

"What IS IT?" Alissa asked.

"IT'S FUCKIN' OWLS! LET ME IN!" Dennis hollered as he got to his feet then ran through the darkness to the tent.

He fumbled with the zipper as his face became assaulted by the talons of the winged attackers.

"MY GOD!" he swatted them away before hurrying into the tent.

The two women sat frozen and wide-eyed, staring at the wounds on his cheeks.

"There are a hundred of them out there!" Dennis said blotting the blood from his face.

A flashlight lit the tent beside them.

"What's going on?" Wes asked.

"There's a fuck-load of owls out there!" Dennis answered.

"WHAT?" Wes repeated.

The tents shook as beating wings and sharp claws assaulted them. They sat in terror of the sudden attack as screeching cries and the sounds of talons shredding canvas echoed through the dark forest. The owls assailed the two-man tents relentlessly, trying to reach the humans hiding within them. The tents swayed against the violent storm of slashing and fluttering. Kelly was screaming, holding onto Alissa. Over the maddening sounds of the owls came a sound distant and hollow. All at once the birds retreated, then went flying into the surrounding woods, their cries echoing off the trees.

The five sat in their battered tents absolutely silent as the scream rang out again.

"The professor!" Wes said.

Wes went out of his tent as cautiously as he could. His flashlight illuminated the dark camp, but all that could be seen of the owls were feathers dancing through the air.

"DR. LIPTON! IS THAT YOU?"

Wes was answered by yet another cry.

"It has to be him!" he said in desperation.

"GET OUT HERE!"

CHAPTER FIVE

Dennis came reluctantly from the tent.

"The girls won't come out," he said.

Wes shined his flashlight in Dennis's direction, studying the scratches on his face.

"The owls," Dennis said.

A scream cut through them, leaving them both shaking.

Wes was obviously rattled.

"Follow me," he said trembling.

They tracked the cries. The night air was crisp and held a chill. Dennis couldn't shake the goose bumps from his skin or the knot in his guts.

The screams came repeatedly from seemingly nearby, yet they could not locate anyone in the darkness.

"It's him, he must be really hurt!" Wes said.

"We have to help him!"

The cries were distinctly human, yet no words could be distinguished. They sought frantically for the professor in all directions by the bright beams of their flashlights.

"DR. LIPTON!" Wes cried.

An agonizingly drawn out scream came in reply as they raced towards it.

At last they discovered a gaping hole of complete darkness.

"Look, a rope!" Dennis pointed out.

"He's down there," Dennis continued. "Maybe he fell and broke his leg or something."

"We have to get down there," Wes breathed, shining his flashlight into the hole.

"I can't see anything up here," he said, before reaching for the rope.

"I'll go down. I have more arm strength," Dennis offered, surprising Wes with his bravery.

"Wait, wait, let's get our plan straight," Wes said, grabbing his arm and holding him there a moment. He was the one in charge, and his conscience couldn't take leading anyone into danger.

"You, me, and then Alissa will go down in that order and Kelly can stay up here with Tyler."

"You're right, he's in no shape to climb in or out and we need to focus on getting the professor out," Dennis agreed.

They went quickly back to the tents to retrieve Alissa. Wes grabbed the professor's pack while Kelly went willingly to sit with Tyler who slept through the entire attack by the owls and still did not awaken.

"Alissa, stay with me!" Kelly begged.

"I can't, Professor Lipton needs me. They need my help," Alissa answered.

"You two will be fine up here," she added.

"I guess it's only a few hours until dawn. We will be ok," Kelly said, in an attempt to calm herself.

****

They stood once more at the edge of the hole with their flashlights pointed down into the unyielding darkness.

"I can't see shit!" Dennis spoke.

"Me neither," Alissa said.

"We've got to get down there, because he sounded like he was in a lot of pain. He could've passed out," Wes said, and reached for the rope only to have Dennis stop him.

"Me first, remember?" Dennis said.

They nodded in agreement as Dennis gripped the rope.

"The professor is old, but he must be in good shape to climb in and out of here."

"He would've used a harness. Where is it?" Wes thought out loud.

Dennis lowered himself down, holding his flashlight in his pocket. As he descended into the hole that was just wide enough to accommodate his thick frame, he could feel the cold, stagnant air engulfing him. A wave of claustrophobia gripped his stomach, but he forced it away.

It was a climb of at least twenty feet. The avid sportsman could feel his arms burning as he made his way slowly down. The rope between his palms bit into his skin, and it felt jagged as if it were comprised of sharp threads of fiberglass. Dennis wondered if Alissa would even be able to make it safely to the stone floor below. His arms shook as his feet fought to gain control of the rope beneath him. The flashlight slid from his pocket, dropping to the cavern bottom. Though it was made to take abuse, it went dark on impact, then clattered across the floor.

"SHIT!" Dennis said through gritted teeth.

"Everything ok?" Wes called down to him.

"I'm fine, just dropped my flashlight," he answered.

"You were supposed to wrap the strap around your wrist so you wouldn't drop it," Alissa said.

"It's a little late for that, Alissa. There is no harness down here," Dennis answered.

Dennis was relieved to finally set foot on the bottom as he released the rope.

Looking up he couldn't see Wes or Alissa, only darkness. He felt his pocket and was relieved to find a Zippo lighter. He thumbed it open, and then with a dry snap it lit, casting a tiny flame. In the utterly blackness of his surroundings it seemed dismal and just about useless, yet it comforted him all the same.

"The harness must've broken. Why'd he go down there alone?" Wes said in frustration.

"I'm coming down!" Alissa called.

"No. I can't risk you falling," Wes said.

"I'm going to be fine," she gripped his shoulder saying. "Professor Lipton needs us."

Wes nodded, and his exhaustion was clear in his face, resigning himself to the fact that he needed all the help he could get in the dire situation.

"Alissa's on her way," Wes called to Dennis.

"Please be cautious," Wes said to her, as she positioned herself before this dark cavity.

"Tell her to be careful, it's harder than it looks," Dennis answered.

"I'm right here and I'm fine," Alissa answered.

"You struggled a bit with the rope yourself, tough guy."

He looked up and saw Alissa inch-worming her way down the rope, anchoring it between her feet to allow her arms to rest as she went. He never answered her, but he knew she was right. Though he was strong, climbing had never been easy for him. Dennis waited for her impatiently. The lighter grew far too hot in his hand, so he blew the flame out, and then slid it back into his pocket. She was there in minutes, but it felt excruciatingly long in the smothering darkness. The absence of light, without moon or stars, without open sky, made him feel as a weight was placed on his chest. Alissa came to rest beside him, her heavy breathing was the only indication of her presence before she flipped on her flashlight. The beam of white light was a small comfort down in the dark hole, but Dennis was thankful for it. Wes was nearly to the bottom when Dennis spotted something in the circle of light cast by Alissa's flashlight.

"Look! A lantern!" Dennis said, his excitement mirrored by Alissa who ran to retrieve it.

"Thank goodness!" She held it up then located the power button on its side.

"Not a crappy old gas one either, it runs on batteries!"

Alissa held it out. The light from the much larger orb engulfed her and was nearly blinding. Dennis came to her side to feel the comfort of it, as it was like a tiny sun she held in her hand.

"We got some other supplies. He was down here," Dennis said.

He rummaged through a pack that was already unzipped. It appeared to be the professor's stash of digging equipment: some trowels, handpicks, small fold-up shovels, brushes, and chisels. He picked up a digital camera, and turned it on to find that no pictures had been taken yet.

"He must have been preparing for our arrival by leaving this stuff here," Alissa said, and her voice held a note of sadness. "I hope he's ok."

Wes set his feet on the damp cave floor just before a scream tore through the silence blanketing them. Wes stumbled back, and then broke his fall by grabbing onto the dangling rope. It slid through his hands, leaving his palms blistered. Dennis wrapped his arms around Wes in an attempt to catch him before he went tumbling over. Wes found the professor's broken harness lying over a jagged rock, with its carabiner clasp broken.

The cavern before them opened up, and then split into several different passages. Alissa caught a glimpse of what appeared to be a man walking away from them and down one of the passages.

"Dr. Lipton?" Alissa said, trying to catch his attention.

"DR. LIPTON?" she repeated, her voice rose and echoed off the stone walls, and then something in her stomach lurched.

"I thought I just saw him!" Alissa pointed in the direction of where she saw the Professor.

"Holy shit, if he's injured he could be disoriented. If he's dehydrated, he could be roaming around down here hopelessly looking for help," Wes said.

Wes was still huffing in exertion from the long climb down.

"What if he got attacked by those nesting owls?" Dennis asked.

The air in the cavern was cool, yet also filled with dust and debris.

"You heard how my voice echoed, so he could be completely confused which way to go," Alissa agreed.

"Come on," Wes said. Alissa and Dennis followed his lead.

They went quickly, yet carefully. The floor was littered with jagged rocks and the ceiling dipped down low in places. Dennis found out by nearly scalping himself at one point, leaving a deep gash on the top of his head. Alissa and Wes walked ahead of him. They jumped as he let loose a string of cuss words, then felt the tender wound on his head, as it bled freely down onto his shirt.

"You ok?" asked Alissa.

"I'm fine," Dennis answered, a little embarrassed.

They continued down the dark passageway, chasing what Alissa thought to be Professor Lipton. They hadn't heard anymore cries and Wes worried the old man could have lost consciousness, then passed out somewhere in the darkness.

"Look, there!" Wes said.

He pointed out a few drops of crimson which were barely detectable against the damp floor. If it weren't for the lantern, they may never have seen them.

"It's blood."

Wes touched the drops before rubbing them between his fingers in the yellow light.

"I bet that he hit his head and is completely confused down here, it makes sense. I feel lost too," Dennis said, speaking his own sense of disorientation aloud.

"It's easy to get turned around in places like this, even if you're an expert."

"I think you're right," Alissa agreed.

They came to a fork in the cave, two passageways led in two different directions. Wes took the lantern from Alissa, then held it out over the ground and located a few more drops of blood. On the wall was a smear of white dust. Chalk.

"He's here, that's how he marked his way. Come on."

****

Tyler's deep breathing nearly lulled Kelly back to sleep. Exhaustion gripped her as she fought to keep her eyes open. The shock of being awakened by the owls left her gut in a tight knot. Kelly listened intently to every sound she heard. The tent was hardly a sanctuary after the attack left it shredded. The echoes of the forest surrounded her, causing her to jump each time anything more than a breeze disturbed the battered shelter. She sat fidgeting and counting the minutes until sunrise. The others had been gone for nearly an hour. Kelly knew because she compulsively checked the watch on her wrist. She desperately clutched at the hopes of hearing their voices upon their return. She lay down beside her injured companion, then slid into Wes's sleeping bag. The forest was coming alive with the approaching dawn, and its busy noises seemed far too loud in her ears. The minutes felt like an eternity as she snuggled closer to Tyler, seeking comfort, hoping he would awaken and chase her terror away with small talk. Kelly knew she had given him an excessive dose of pain killers. She guessed he would probably sleep like he was in a coma. She wished she hadn't been so generous with her medication. A snapping of dry wood in the distance sent her scooting even closer to Tyler. Kelly could feel his hot breath on her face and it eased her mind a bit to know he hadn't overdosed the night before. She kept herself far from the tattered walls of the tent, then pulled the sleeping bag up over her head to hide. Kelly heard it again. She held her breath. Though the air felt chill outside, the inside of the sleeping bag grew stifling with her deep breathing. What she heard next was very distinct, and she fought back the urge to weep. Kelly felt all alone lying beside Tyler, as something approached. She didn't want to believe it, but she had to, because the flutter of wings was unmistakable.

****

The passage wound around, then snaked back beneath the mountain. Dennis couldn't help but feel the sense of being buried alive. He never felt such an intense sensation in all of his life and mentally he struggled to proceed deeper into the caverns. The feeling of suffocation gripped him again, refusing to be forced back. They followed a blood trail for over an hour. It took them down many offshoots and side passages. Dennis was trying to keep a mental map of each time they took a left or a right. He felt now completely lost and at the mercy of the mountain above him. The feeling of being entombed alive was at an unbearable level as he huffed, trying desperately to fill his lungs.

"I don't know how much further I can go," he admitted.

"I know what you mean, it's hard to breathe down here," Alissa said.

"LOOK!" Wes said.

Ahead of them appeared to be a line of faint light.

"What is it?" Dennis asked, his voice sounding tense.

In the light of the lantern Alissa could see he had broken out in a sweat.

"Is the path too tight?"

"NO! LOOK!" Wes grabbed the flashlight, then directed its beam to the passageway before them, illuminating a set of stone doors that had been forced open.

"The doorway," Wes's voice fell to a whisper.

Beyond the opening came a faint light. Wes rushed forward to examine the doorway, but Alissa and Dennis hesitated. The blood trail that they had been following now appeared to end unexpectedly.

"Do you think the professor went in there?" Dennis asked.

"The blood trail stopped."

Alissa could feel her hackles raise, as his question was valid. The situation made no sense to her. Had they been following the dripping blood of a man who had wandered around confused through passageways? Had he been disoriented for hours before they discovered this camp and cavernous pit?

"Dennis is right. The professor must've been here awhile," Alissa said.

"He probably slipped down another passage and out of our sight before we realized it. He could be anywhere!"

Wes turned to answer her as a moan from the other side of the doorway froze him before he could speak. He turned slowly back to shine the flashlight into the opening.

"Hello? Professor Lipton?" he said, though his voice shook with uncertainty.

There was no answer.

He took a step closer as Alissa rushed forward to grab his arm.

"Wait."

She couldn't say why she held him back, but something deep in her gut was now screaming for her to run, to get out as fast as she could. Alissa felt embarrassed by the look on his face as the wave of alarm passed.

"Sounds carry weird in places like this," Wes said. "It could've been the wind coming through a hole down the tunnel."

Alissa released him as he advanced. His flashlight drifted over the elaborately carved doorway. Hieroglyphics were visible and upon the ground was the evidence of the professor's work, a hand pick and brush. Wes studied the carvings that had been cleaned of centuries of dirt and grime. He recognized many of the glyphs.

"What is it?" Dennis asked.

CHAPTER SIX

The tent was assailed by the birds once more. Kelly retreated deeper into the sleeping bag. She held her breath, not wishing to excite them with her screams. The canvas ripped again beneath their talons and she wondered if Tyler would ever awaken. She was being driven crazy by the screeching. Kelly dared to slip one of her hands out to shake Tyler, but again she didn't get a response from him. Inside of the sleeping bag it became stifling with her gasping breaths. She felt as if she would surely suffocate before the episode came to an end. The silence that followed was nerve racking, for she could feel something waiting, something watching. All she could hear now was her own heavy breathing, but the sobs she had choked back were now uncontainable. Kelly wept while reaching her hand out to shake Tyler once more. He didn't respond and Kelly worried if she had actually put him into a coma with the handful of pills she had helped him swallow. Kelly only brought her medication just in case her knee got sore from the hike, not to immobilize her only protection from a flock of enraged birds. She crept out of the sleeping bag. She was relieved to think dawn was approaching. It calmed Kelly momentarily until she noticed the shadows outside. Dozens of owl shapes sat waiting, keeping vigil over the tent in which she hid. Kelly slapped her hand over her mouth to hold back the frightened cries escaping through her fingers.

The shadows beyond the useless tent stretched and pulled, morphing into human-like figures. She turned to see Tyler stirring in his sleep.

"WAKE UP!" Kelly cried.

She froze when she felt its presence behind her. She knew she had been found out. She could no longer hide. A hand reached through a gaping hole in the tent to grip her shoulder and tears filled her eyes. Kelly couldn't bring herself to turn around, to see the identity of the shadow that could transform from bird to man.

****

"It's a depiction of Xibalba," Wes spoke.

Dennis had no idea what Xibalba was but it didn't sound good.

"What?"

"The Mayan underworld, or the place of fear," Wes answered.

"Here it tells of their journey, the shadows of death following them and killing them one by one."

Wes turned and looked to Alissa as Dennis snatched the flashlight.

"The owl is a symbol of death."

"I'm getting out of here!" Dennis said.

"Dennis, WAIT!" Alissa said.

He was already retreating back up the black cavern. It was clear he wouldn't come back.

"DENNIS!"

****

The skeletal fingers released Kelly's shoulder before winding their way violently into her hair. They yanked her backwards through the battered tent wall. She emerged in the dim light, the sun hadn't risen completely, and her heart sank. Kelly fought the fingers tangled in her hair, sinking her nails deep into a wrist attached to the hand. She rolled onto her back to see her attacker. A skeletal figure, its skin hung in fetid layers. The flesh had peeled back from its face, revealing the skull beneath. What was left of the long, dark hair clinging to its skull was adorned with feathers, the feathers of an owl. Its eyes were much too large for its face and golden like those of the bird. Plumes of grey and white feathers hung from the decaying flesh of the creature's naked and sexless body. It parted its thin, dry lips and screeched. In moments a crowd of other owl creatures, all misshapen and unnatural, flapped and fluttered about Kelly, tearing her clothes from her body. They sunk their talons into her flesh and bore her up off of the ground. She screamed as she was carried beyond the campsite, then dangled over a man-size hole in the earth. Kelly thought they would surely drop her into the unfathomable pit and her stomach leapt into her throat.

They held her there before slowly lowering her into the blinding darkness, gripping her arms and legs and stretching them painfully outward. The wounds inflicted by the piercing claws of the creatures bled and stung mercilessly and each time Kelly writhed to break free, they only sunk deeper into her burning flesh. As she was suspended, a cry signaling an instruction let loose and they began cutting the skin from her body. Her nerves were raw. It felt as if she had been dowsed with gasoline and set on fire. Tears ran from Kelly's eyes, her lungs and throat burned from crying out helplessly. Every inch of her skin was pulled taut and removed with talons as sharp as scalpels. Bile rose in Kelly's throat as the agony persisted, drowning out her cries in gurgling and gagging. The only flesh spared was on her hands and feet. The last thing she felt was talons seizing the skin along her jawline.

****

Tyler drifted in a near comatose state, dreaming of owls and someone screaming.

****

Dennis knew they had walked for hours within the underground cave system, taking random passageways in hopes of locating the Professor. He was aware it was not a good idea to take off on his own, but his terror had gotten the best of him. He found himself armed with nothing but a flashlight. He stopped in midstride as screams echoed down the cavern to him and instantly he regretted his decision to leave his companions. Dennis wondered if he should return to Wes and Alissa. The cries died and by the sound of them he judged the distance to be much farther away from him than Wes and Alissa. Dennis wondered from where the wails came. He couldn't decide which way to go, but the need to get out of the caves became priority. Dennis's claustrophobia took over, urging him to continue in his current direction hoping he could find the entryway to the cavern. His lungs felt constricted and dizzying nausea gripped his gut like a vice. Dennis continued shakily, praying to find the way back into the fresh air that was now above him through tons of soil and rock. There was a low rumble in the mountain, dust danced in his eyes. He felt as if he would surely suffocate. His brain told him that at any minute he would be buried alive, the ceiling would give away, and he would be crushed. Dennis took off with all of the speed he could afford, his flashlight beam bouncing wildly, and its light seemed insignificant now. The stone walls grew narrow and encroaching as if they were great mouths slowly swallowing him. Dennis stumbled over a pile of stones, then came down hard upon his knees. The skin peeled back on the jagged rocks as he impacted the damp floor. He was winded and fought to breathe. He pulled himself to his feet once more before rushing forward in the direction of where the screams had died, leaving the caves silent and still. The sense of urgency within Dennis was building into a full blown panic attack.

****

Alissa stood there looking over Wes's shoulder at the cryptic hieroglyphics. She worried about Dennis and could feel her own anxiety growing.

"What's that?" she asked the associate professor, pointing to a depiction of what appeared to be half-human and half-beast holding a severed head.

"The Wayob, a demon of sorts, myths stated it had shapeshifting abilities," Wes answered.

"And that?" Alissa's hand ran over the carving of a man with a bloated body and the head of an owl.

Wes studied it beneath the lantern light yet didn't speak a word for a long time. Alissa looked to him for the answer he seemed reluctant to give and it concerned her.

"That is Ah-Puch, others called him Cisin. He is the Lord of Death," Wes spoke at last.

The elaborately carved doorway was missing the disc to be placed in its center. There was still a faint light flickering beyond it but she couldn't bring herself to look inside. Her skin prickled as the hair on her neck rose, something in her gut told her she needed to run.

"I don't like this. I want to go back to camp."

"We can't go back until we find the professor," Wes answered, his eyes still examining the ancient door.

"I really want to go back!" Alissa said.

"Once we have found Dr. Lipton we can get out of here. We can't just leave him down here. We saw him...you saw him!"

Alissa stood for a minute and reined in her anxiety.

She nodded. "Let's find him and then get out of here."

Wes stood for a moment longer, then abruptly turned away from the door.

"Let's go!"

They returned to their search as Wes went quickly along.

"We have to catch up with Dennis," Wes said.

"Fuckin' idiot might get lost down here too," she said, as she struggled to keep up.

****

Dennis knew by the narrowing of the tunnel that he had taken a wrong turn. He stopped to catch his breath and it felt as if his lungs were only working at half capacity. He worried if there would be enough air to keep him conscious. Dennis turned back then began tracing his steps back to his former location. He prayed he could just find the way back to the hole. He would climb out of there as fast as his arms could manage.

107

Before him another scream came echoing down the passageway to greet his stomach with a fist of cold fear. Dennis froze, and behind him the tunnel had grown so tight he had to turn sideways to navigate it, yet before him resounded those god-awful cries. They were shrill, long and drawn out, but as suddenly as they began, they ended. He decided to continue tracing his steps in the hopes of finding Alissa and Wes. The flashlight in his hand flickered, making his heart pound.

"Don't you fuckin' die!" Dennis spoke down to it, his voice shook.

"Please! No!"

The passageway went black, then the old feeling of being buried alive multiplied a hundred fold. Dennis slapped the flashlight against his palm and cussed. His voice sounded amplified in his ears as he choked back his second string of dirty words. The urgency to get the flashlight to work, to have the comfort of its miniscule light, made his hands shake. Dennis struggled to untwist the cap, as he thought if he rotated the batteries maybe it would work once more. He dumped the batteries out into his hand but lost one in the darkness that was enveloping him and it clattered loudly upon the cave floor.

"GODDAMNIT!"

Dennis fell to his knees searching for the lost battery. His hands ran through a damp pool and he remembered his lighter. He threw the flashlight to the ground, then reached into his pocket to locate the Zippo. He was trembling as he flicked it open and his heart lurched before its small flame jumped to life. The momentary blindness from its sudden illumination faded and he noticed his sticky, wet hands were covered in a black putrid liquid.

His eyes roved beyond inspecting his hands to see bare feet before him, shins bound so tight with leather that it bit into the splitting skin where shards of bone were barely contained. The flesh was pale and bloodless, crudely painted with blue pigment. Dennis's eyes followed the length of the body, taking in the walking corpse. Black blood hung in thick strings from the vicious wounds. A steady drip fell from an opened abdomen. Dennis's nose was assaulted by a foul odor, which caused him to gag. He fell back onto his ass, one hand held the lighter out before him. His gaze drifted up beyond the open cavities in the corpse's belly and chest and came to rest on its face. Its eyes were now widened black pits filled with those of a different beast and they were the same he had seen glowing beneath the light of the moon--the eyes of an owl.

****

The thing that was once the Professor cocked its head to one side, studying its prey before it.

"Professor?" the human said. "Professor, please!"

He shambled awkwardly forward on his damaged legs, reaching for the next sacrifice to be broken over the stone and have his heart removed. The Lord of Death awaited, Xibalba awaited. The human held a tiny flame in his hand, but as the creature wailed down in his face, it was snuffed out.

****

Tyler opened his eyes. The intense need to vomit gripped his stomach. He sat forward as it flew from his mouth in an almost volcanic explosion, both in velocity and heat. The stench of it hung in his nose, and it left the back of his throat feeling acidic. He looked down to see he had soiled his sleeping bag along with his clothes. Embarrassment burned in his face as he absent-mindedly attempted to wipe the mess away. A surge of overwhelming pain forced him to remember his tumble down the mountainside. Tyler's arm was still bound to his chest in a sling made from Dennis's shirt. The many scrapes about his body were beginning to scab over and stick to his clothing. It took him a great while to extricate his legs from the sleeping bag before crawling clumsily forward. He climbed out of the shredded tent, taking care not to bump his aching arm. He stumbled as if in a drunken stupor and his mind still felt muddled. He remembered Kelly feeding him painkillers, his stomach balled into an aching knot. He leaned forward and dry-heaved. His stomach was empty but his body still attempted to force the remainder of the medication from his system. He had never been so nauseated even after the all-night parties he regularly attended where his drink of choice was whiskey. His abdomen began to cramp with violent spasms. He sat down on a fallen tree desperately trying to pull himself together, but the churning in his gut wouldn't cease.

The camp was empty. He assumed the others had gone to look for the Professor. He was grateful to be alone, as he didn't want anyone to see him bent over with tears running down his cheeks as he dry-heaved and prayed for his torment to end. The nausea waned and he was overcome with relief. Tyler looked about through watery eyes. He still didn't see any of his companions, and it made him wonder as he smelled himself how he would change his vomit-soaked clothing with only one functional arm. When they returned, he would swallow his pride and beg Kelly to assist him. The forest was full of the sounds of the breeze through the trees, insects humming about, and in the distance, there was a hoot. His anger with the bird was silenced by thoughts of the foolishness of his actions and those that ended up nearly killing him. Tyler's arm throbbed incessantly as the pain was soon becoming almost unbearable. The desperate need to make his agony go away made him run his hand roughly through his hair and grit his teeth. Though they made him sick, he knew he needed more of Kelly's painkillers, and he figured she wouldn't mind if he helped himself to a few more. Tyler stood shakily before he began making his way back to the tent. His clouded mind never noticed how battered the campsite was until he caught a sight that almost made him forget his agony.

Out beyond the edge of camp, she stood with her back to him, naked in the morning sunlight. Kelly must have stayed behind to care for him. What a pleasant way to ease his pain. He hadn't noticed her before and it made him grin at the thoughts of the little game she was playing with him...a sensual little game.

He decided to play along so he made his way slowly and silently across the camp. He stopped, glancing down at his filthy clothes.

"Not very sexy," Tyler muttered to himself.

He still felt half-stoned from painkillers as he unbuttoned his shorts with his good hand and yanked them down along with his underwear, stumbling out of them as he resumed his approach, watching her walking into the tree line. The thoughts of having a tumble with her in the forest coaxed him to quicken his pace. He could feel himself growing excited with the thoughts of lying her down and letting her medicine heal his wounds.

He passed the tree line and spoke.

"Nurse Kelly! I need your special kind of healing!"

She didn't answer, but he knew she had to have heard him. In the distance he caught a glimpse of her pale hand and shoulder. Tyler quickened his steps, feeling his arousal soar.

"I need you, baby," he said.

"Come take my pain away."

He felt something other than his arm throbbing. Ahead of him he caught another glimpse of her.

"Don't run away, baby!" his voice echoed through the now silent forest.

He was clothed in only a pair of socks, tennis shoes, and a puke-stained shirt, but embarrassment didn't even come to mind as he crept between the trees. If there were any hikers around, he planned on giving them quite the show.

"I need a sponge bath," he teased.

Tyler found her standing with her back to him once more and he recalled the night he watched her step out of the creek, her breasts full and perky. He couldn't contain his urges anymore, he needed to feel her. He walked with his good hand outstretched; he reached for her silken shoulder when his blurry eyes noticed her legs were filthy and her hair was a ratted mess. Jealousy burned in him and he wondered if Dennis hadn't got to have her first. His hand rested on Kelly's shoulder and she felt ice cold.

"Hey, Kell, what's wrong?" Tyler asked.

The feeling radiating from her definitely was not playful or sexy and it worried him. His manhood shrunk back and hung there in disappointment and concern. She turned to face him as he realized her hands were not the same and the dark substance clinging to her legs was dried blood.

"Kelly?" he whispered.

Tyler backed away when she turned to face him and he caught a glimpse of what once was her face and torso. There were long lacerations running the length of her body from her collarbone down to her pubic bone, and they looked like claw marks. There were also puncture wounds dotting her skin, and by their spacing it made him think they were caused by talons penetrating her flesh. Tyler guessed her bones weren't even beneath her skin, for within the long cuts appeared to writhe the flesh of something else. Kelly's face and hair hung like a cheap mask over a misshapen head. There were holes torn in her skin to accommodate the large golden eyes now peering at him. Tyler tumbled then rolled across the lichen-blanketed ground. It was the color of blood. His injured arm was useless in his attempt to escape, only adding to his distress. He kicked as the creature lurched forward, knocking the Kelly mask loose. It hung for a moment from sticky strands that glued her lifeless flesh to the hideous face beneath. It fell to the ground revealing the monster's true visage. Its humanoid head twitched and it cried out, a long piercing screech. It studied him for a moment before bending to retrieve a large jagged stone. Tyler knew its intent and rolled to his knees in an attempt to gain his footing to run. He felt the sharp blow of the projectile as it hit him in the back of his knees causing his legs to buckle. He fell roughly upon his good hand and he heard a snap of his wrist. The pain was instant yet he hadn't the time to acknowledge it for he was bludgeoned yet again with another stone. It stood over him, clutching a jagged, heavy rock in its hands. Each time it was brought down into his flesh Tyler could hear his meat

being severed and torn. He screamed but there was no one
to hear his cries for help.

CHAPTER SEVEN

Wes was silent. Alissa could see his jaw was clinched in the lantern light. They came to a fork in the passageway and he hesitated, listening. He pulled her along, his pace increasing with each passing minute.

"What was on that door?" she asked.

He didn't answer.

"What did you see that made you so...afraid?"

"I have been thinking about the glyphs, the meaning of them. They tell a story," he said, then halted for a moment.

"There was a group that came to settle here but death followed them." His voice dropped until it was barely audible.

"It was sealed beyond that door by the bloodletting of a priestess. It was not famine or sickness like I originally thought."

"What was sealed here?" said Alissa.

"Ah-Puch and Xibalba."

Alissa's face was blank and he knew she didn't fully understand.

"Death... and Hell," Wes said.

****

Dennis fought back, kicking out at the walking corpse of Dr. Lipton. His heel made contact with a leather-bound shin bone, breaking a splinter off. The putrid shell of the Professor fell upon him with its cold hands seeking his throat. They struggled with each other violently. Dennis was shocked by the strength of the corpse on top of him. Dennis screamed as chipped nails found the scratches in his cheek and dug into the claw marks left by the owls, peeling away his flesh from his face in thin strips. A blast of a conch shell stopped the attack and Dennis struggled to his feet, intent on running. He dropped his lighter in the attack and was surrounded by utter darkness. A second blast rattled him, and it was followed by a ragged breath behind him. He knew the Professor was the least of his worries.

****

They were running down the tunnels at full speed. Alissa began to think Wes's intent was only to make it to the rope and abandon the professor and Dennis. Shamefully, she didn't stop him, as all Alissa wanted was to be in the open air and far away from the cavern. A blast from some kind of horn came echoing down the dark cavern. Wes froze, pulling her tightly against him. They held their breath in disbelief. A second blast came to greet their trembling bodies, it was unmistakable.

"It's impossible," he whispered.

"Impossible."

****

Dennis couldn't see the figure in the darkness, but it stood behind him. Ah-Puch. Or as otherwise known, the master of the dead who commanded all the demons of the underworld. He could see the human through his eyes, those of a nocturnal hunter. His hair hung from his decrepit scalp in matted chunks, adorned with tiny bells. Dennis could hear their faint sound yet he couldn't force himself to turn in their direction. The stench of the Lord of Death gave away the certainty of his presence, since it was of pure decay and smoke. Dennis spun but his eyes couldn't discern a thing. A sharp pain erupted in his throat, and he brought his hand up to the object lodged there. The knife felt like a jagged shard of stone as he reflexively tried to swallow around it. Dennis's blood came out in a fountain once it was yanked free, and it left a gaping slit destroying his esophagus and puncturing an artery. With each beat of his racing heart, his blood spilled out onto the cave floor. He attempted to stem its flow by squeezing his neck closed with his own hands, but he knew death was imminent when the dagger was driven into his gut so far he felt its tip nick his spine.

****

Tyler found it impossible to drag himself forward. His legs were beaten into useless and bloody meat by the monster that wore Kelly's skin. He was ravaged again; this time his lower back was the target of large stones. He cried out, coughing up bile as he struggled to pull himself further until the air erupted in a fury of beating wings and screeching. Tyler rolled over. Above him had gathered an unimaginable sight, as the sky was filled with hundreds of misshapen owls, all with clawed fingers on the tips of their wings, human-like feet with sharp talons, and oversized heads with great golden eyes. Their cries were distorted now almost as if they came from human vocal cords, a mockery of the natural bird's calls. They came swooping and slashing at his flesh. A handful of them began scooping up stones in their elongated feet to drop down upon him.

The sounds of his bones snapping and a nauseating pain filled his consciousness. Though he fought to get to his feet, to stand and run, he couldn't rise against the hail of stones pummeling his already hopelessly broken body. The barrage of rocks decimated his once powerful frame. Tyler's head spun as a flurry of feathers and agonizing pain swallowed him up.

****

"What is that?" Alissa dared to whisper.

Wes clamped his hand roughly over her mouth. "SHHH!"

She nodded her head and Wes released her. Alissa knew she had heard screaming, and then the second sound, the blast of a horn was unmistakable. The silence around them was suffocating, and though the lantern was comforting, she wondered then if they should turn it off. Wes glanced back behind them and she could almost read his thoughts. He did not want to return to the doorway with the pale light beyond it, yet the blast of some kind of horn hindered them from taking another step forward. Alissa held in the questions she felt so desperate to ask for fear that someone or something would hear her voice. They stood there listening to their stifled breathing that echoed off the stone walls around them.

She looked to him, and her face seemed to ask "What's next?" and all he could do was shake his head in terrified confusion. Wes's hands trembled as he reached over and pressed the button on the lantern, leaving them in complete darkness.

****

Tyler's skin became nothing more than a fleshy bag serving to hold his fractured and splintering bones. His moaning grew weak from the last assault and his damaged lungs barely drew enough breath to continue. The creature wearing Kelly's skin suit heaved Tyler painfully over its shoulder before making its way back to the hole in the earth. Tyler's broken arms swayed uselessly back and forth with the motion of the monster's strides. It wasn't large by any means, but it was muscular and bore his weight without exertion. The others followed along in their bloody trail, some still in bird form, while a handful hopped along morphed somewhere between man and owl. A long bloody string of spittle dripped from between Tyler's lips. The back of his head had been half caved in by the blow of a heavy stone. He was dying when he was held out over the hole. Somewhere in his swollen brain registered the grave danger, yet his soul welcomed death. He made not a sound as he was released, the breath caught in his throat at the sudden drop, an involuntary reaction. Tyler met the stone floor with such force that it split his gut in a wet smack. The Wayobs fell in upon him in a cloud of feathers.

****

Alissa held him tight. His arms were hardly a comfort in the darkness with nowhere to run. Wes pushed her slowly back in the direction they had come, and in the far distance, the light beyond the doorway looked like a tiny line. She watched as it began to pulse and grow brighter. Wes too noticed the change and hesitated. The illumination rippled and beyond its reach drifted a cold current that came spilling out the opened doorway. He held her hand and stepped towards it. Alissa tugged him back, shaking her head. In the glow creeping to them slowly, she could see him hold his finger against his lips. Wes could sense how badly she wished to scream and attempted to calm her. He released her hand then walked towards the light. She found herself completely alone. Alissa hurried after him though her instincts told her it was far from a sane idea.

****

Dennis was dragged along by his ankles. He was steadily bleeding out and his breathing echoed in a sickly gurgling about him. The vision of what appeared to be some dark shaman walked before him. Dennis's face was raw and the musty air that found its way into his lungs through his shallow breathing tasted of rot. He could feel the skin on his back being rubbed raw and shredding against the rough stone floor as he was pulled along. The eviscerated Professor staggered along behind them, his abdomen looked like a gaping mouth. His body was already beginning to decay. Dennis knew death was near and he hoped he would drift away into a land of unconsciousness. He prayed his blood loss would claim him long before the monster could fulfill whatever cruel plans it had for his flesh. He remembered the story that Wes told Alissa about the Lord of Death and he knew his torment would not be swift.

****

The blasting of the conch shell kept the dead lingering within their broken bodies, a cruel trick of Ah-Puch. The Lord of Death would not release them until he was satisfied with their torment. Kelly's corpse stood and walked along in the darkness. Her skin had been removed and she was slick with blood. She made a wet, groaning noise as she made her way down the black passageways. The master of death called to her and she would answer him. The blast of a conch shell rattled her skull as it passed through her open nasal cavity, as her nose had been removed along with her heavy breasts that once bounced upon her chest. She cried out, an unearthly call. The Lord of Xibalba beckoned her forth, a walking corpse to her new home within the lands of the dead.

****

The sound met them, a wet, sliding noise. Alissa could hardly contain her cries and had to stifle them back. Wes spun to listen, and hurriedly he pushed her towards the stone doorway. Alissa shook her head then fought against him.

He brought his lips close to her ear. "GO! Something is coming!"

She stood still, unable to force herself to move.

"GO!"

Alissa was pushed along in front of him. The light before them was growing brighter and the wind carrying those faint voices swept over them, growing into a chorus of distressed screams. Tears fell down her cheeks. They were trapped between two unknowns. Alissa moved slowly, gripping his hand as they proceeded together They had no options left.

They stopped before the doorway. The glyphs were illuminated. She watched his eyes as he studied them. A frantic confusion tightened his face as if he was searching for the significance of them. The opening pulsed a blue light, and Wes squeezed her hand then pulled her forward. Alissa couldn't help but squint into its brilliance as the stench of rotting flesh met her nostrils.

CHAPTER EIGHT

Wes took Alissa by the hand as they stepped through the ancient doors and into the antechamber before them, both desperately wishing to avoid whatever was coming down the passageway at their backs. Skeletal remains lay before them like a morbid signpost announcing they had stepped into the land of the dead. Their nostrils were filled with the stink of centuries-old decay. Beyond where they stood was a set of crumbling stone steps and they hurried over and down to hide behind a set of massive stone pillars resting on their sides. Everything was overgrown with creeping thorny vines that appeared to be either dead or going into permanent dormancy. A roadway of flat stone met the end of the stairs leading to a massive pyramid taking up the very heart of the mountain above them. Dying forests surrounded it; there at its back cascaded a waterfall. The walls of the enormous cavern were pocked with many caves, causing it to look like a honeycomb of black stone. High above them smoldered a circle of indigo flame like a faint blue halo, casting an illumination much like moonlight. Wes gripped Alissa's mouth closed before pulling her down to the ground where they lay in hiding beneath a veil of thorns, awaiting the passing of the source of the commotion now filling the antechamber above them. A whimpering steadily grew into gurgled crying, which they recognized to be Dennis's voice. Their view was partially obscured by the vines momentarily, but as the procession came into view Alissa began to weep beneath Wes's hand trying to hold her silent. She could feel him at her back as he cried too. Dennis was pulled by his ankles down the stone steps, as Professor Lipton, on shattered leg bones, tugged one foot, and his belly hanging agape like the black gill of a dead fish. Pulling their helpless companion by his other foot was a figure Wes had seen in many books on Mayan beliefs, Ah-Puch, the Lord of Xibalba. He had a head like a deformed owl, and his body was bloated and stinking with death's signature. In their trail followed a figure of raw flesh, its blood coagulating in the musty cavern air, though it held no trace of its former identity as its petite frame appeared feminine. Alissa knew in her heart the skinless one was Kelly. The Wayobs came flying through the cavern

130

mouth in a storm of feathers with their humanoid faces adorned with great beaks. They were all screeching, and in their talon-tipped feet they bore Tyler whose body was broken and twisted out of ordinary human shape. He hung limp beneath them, blood ran from his mouth and opened abdomen to adorn those in the line with crimson rain. The Lord of Death called to the lead Wayob who still wore the tattered skin of Kelly's face like a mask over its own hideous visage which brought Alissa to nauseating hysteria. It came to present Tyler to its master who inspected his tribute, and satisfied, he continued to lead the procession to the great pyramid before them, akin to a primitive Pied Piper. He beckoned them forth to claim their flesh and souls. Torches of blue flame numbering in the hundreds leaped to life as the train of the damned passed, illuminating the ruins and broken monuments about the temple's base, then climbing up each step of the pyramid. The inhabitants of the underworld came creeping from an eroded city, handfuls of putrefied dead. Some were adorned like kings; they were obviously high-ranking denizens. They watched in grizzly delight as the fresh flesh was paraded by them. They were stained Mayan Blue, gruesomely cheering, hailing their ruler in the tongue of a long deceased and scattered civilization.

****

They lay in the darkness of the vines. Wes felt a pricking at his skin, something tightly gripped his ankle. He stifled a scream as he realized the thorn bushes were now moving and slowly attempting to wrap about them. The barbs were about the size of those on a rose bush and with each wound they opened they seemed to move with more ferocity. They were yearning for the blood of the living. He forced Alissa out of the plants' grip as the thorns began to sink into his skin like the teeth of a hidden predator. He tore them free, leaving small puncture wounds. She covered her mouth, trying not to scream as she watched him struggle to break loose. Once they were clear of the vampire vines, Wes turned to see the exit and antechamber being covered by more of them, a legion of thirsty foliage slithered together to form an impenetrable doorway, waiting for the humans to try to escape so that they would become entangled like flies in a spider web. Wes knew they couldn't attempt it. They would be engulfed and slowly bled dry. Alissa joined him to gaze for a long while in horrified hopelessness, and they were trapped in the land of fear. They turned their attention to their companions who were ascending the steps of the pyramid temple.

"We have to get out of here," Alissa whispered.

Wes looked to her, frantically placing his finger to his lips in an attempt to silence her. The thoughts of drawing attention to themselves had already knotted his gut with fear. She crossed her arms over her chest, waiting for him to answer. Wes stepped close to her ear before speaking.

"What about the others?" Wes asked.

Alissa looked to them, so far way, drawn to their doom by the enchantment of the master of death.

"They are already gone. You saw them too. They are dead, but screaming, blinking and walking." Her voice shook as tears wet her cheeks.

Wes nodded, knowing no matter how much her words hurt they were the truth. In his studies it told that anything living that entered Xibalba would also die slowly. As they stood there he knew they were dying too. He looked into Alissa's eyes, he couldn't tell her.

"One of these caves must lead out," he said softly.

Alissa studied the multitude of openings in the cavern walls and dismay seized her heart.

"Which one should we choose then?" she asked.

"Let's start here," Wes said, and pointed to a black hole not far from them.

****

"Turn on the light," Wes whispered, after they had blindly stumbled into the tight entryway. They felt their way along a distance in the dark to assure their light source wouldn't be like a signal to the spectral hunters of Xibalba. Alissa pressed the button on the battery-powered lantern she still gripped in her shaking hand, then passed it over to Wes. The sudden illumination was a shock, leaving their vision invaded by dancing red dots. Wes took off the professor's pack, and unzipped it. His hand felt the heavy disc inside. He knew it had to be useless unless they too wanted to cut their own throats. He shivered looking up at her hopeful face, unwilling to give up until he fought to bring Alissa back to the land of the living. He found two waist harnesses with a lead rope that he attached between them. Wes shoved the disc back into the bottom of the pack.

He helped Alissa step into one harness before slipping into one himself.

"This isn't really what these are made for but at least we don't lose one another."

After they adjusted the harnesses they moved onward slowly. The walls grew closer and closer together until they were barely able to squeeze between them while walking sideways. Alissa could feel the grip of claustrophobia tightening about her throat, nervous sweat tracing lines down her sides. She knew the air in the world above would be crisp, even chilly against her skin; it would fill her lungs with deep breaths of approaching autumn. However, in the lands below is where she found herself, fighting to breath within the tomb she had entered willingly. The cold within the cavern was not born of changing seasons but of looming death, and it pressed against her chest, threatening to suffocate her. Alissa looked to Wes whose face was grim with the determination to live, but she knew in his heart he too felt the mountain above them was nothing more than a closed casket lid. She fought back the urge to cry, as she knew it wouldn't have eased the tumult of emotions that were building inside of her of sadness, grief, hopelessness, and anger which all combined into a disastrous cocktail of defeat.

"It gets wider a little further up!" Wes said, and she could hear an ounce of hope in his voice.

Alissa didn't expect to find a door with a red exit sign hung above it, but the thoughts of the stone walls receding back to a comfortable distance helped ease her anxiety. The jagged rocks at her back were biting into the tender flesh above her buttocks. Warmth ran down into her pants and she knew she was bleeding; the mountain was slowly devouring her. Alissa fought her way through without any care of the wounds she might inflict upon herself. She needed to feel the open space Wes had spotted ahead of them. After a final push, she found herself standing next to Wes in an open chamber. The feeling of being suffocated abated to an acceptable degree as she stood beside him breathing heavily. It was obvious Wes felt relieved if only a little bit. He began walking the perimeter of the stone room, searching for any other openings.

"Come this way," he said.

Alissa took two steps across the room to where his voice seemed to originate before feeling the floor suddenly nonexistent beneath her feet. Her arms shot out as her body twisted in midair gripping and missing the jagged edge of the hole which she had walked right into. The lead rope pulled her roughly against the chasm's edge. Her chin hit the sharp stone ledge, busting it wide open. Her glasses tumbled from her face before falling into the black void beneath her. The sound of their impact upon the bottom of the pit only registered in her ears as a small *tink* below her cries for help.

"Hold on!" Wes yelled.

He had instinctively pitched forward when he felt her falling, and her weight nearly dragged him over the edge. His hands gripped the stones on the floor, and deep gouges were cut into his arms and elbows as he fought to save them both. The tug on the rope lessened as she grabbed a hold of the side of the hole, pulling herself up to the edge, frantically screaming. He managed to get to his knees, then shakily made his way to her.

"Hold on," he urged her.

He crawled towards the lantern lying on its side before him as he quickly made his way to the edge of the void. She looked as if she was being swallowed alive when he located her at last. Wes left the lantern on the floor as he grabbed her by her arm and helped tug her back to safety. He held their light source over the hole to see it span most of the cavern, but for a four-foot ledge about its rim, the path Wes had been lucky enough to follow.

"That's why I walked the edge. I thought you would do the same."

Alissa didn't answer, she only lay there shaking and bleeding from the deep wound on her chin.

"Only follow my exact path from now on. Please, I can't do this alone," he said.

She nodded in response as he sat beside her, squeezing her shoulder in an effort to comfort her as tears fell from her eyes.

****

The view from the top of the temple showed a vast, dark kingdom of ruin and decay. Dennis could see it all from where he was lying. Tyler was very obviously already dead, yet his eyes stared up at the blue light above them. The Professor stood gutted beside him, waiting like an obedient dog. Kelly walked without her skin in a trance-like state, and he knew if she had been fully conscious every pain receptor in her brain would be screaming in agony. He was still bleeding, though the rush of blood had stemmed to a drip. He had bled to death, yet he found himself conscious. Dennis recalled what Wes had said about the Mayan underworld and he knew that he had found himself there, in a hell where death would not release him from suffering. The thing that brought them to his lands of death stood looking down upon the crowds of decrepit walking corpses and laughing demon kings. The owl creatures fluttered to perch on the steps below him. Dennis could not decipher the words the monster spoke with a guttural voice, but it incited them to cheer, and then dance with macabre. Though Dennis was trying to remain quiet and absolutely still, he cried out when a flying creature landed before the beast once its speech seemed to come to an end. It wore a face as a mask, Kelly's sweet angelic visage with bloodied edges, and that's when Dennis realized it had breasts...not breasts of its own, but it wore Kelly's tanned skin like a suit stretched over its own deformed body, morphed into something between man and bird, with its feathers protruding through her soft skin. The Lord of the Dead laughed at his terror, then turned to Kelly who was standing beside Professor Lipton. He wrapped his hand around her throat before lifting her up before him. The pale blue crowd at the bottom of the temple went wild, reaching their boney hands up to him as he let Kelly dangle above the steep steps. They began chanting in a frenzy of anticipation as he carried her to a large stone, then ceremoniously he bent her backwards over it before the Owl men came to hold her in place. Dennis looked on as a stone dagger was placed in Ah-Puch's hand. He held the obsidian blade up, causing the onlookers to roar with excitement. He brought it down into Kelly's breast bone, and a short cry escaped her lipless mouth. The dagger was heavy and used more to crush her ribcage than for actually slicing, as he thrust it outward and to the side to open a fist-sized hole there. The lord of the dead thrust his hand inside, gripped her still beating heart, then yanked it free to present it to his legion. Blood ran down his arm as he held it aloft. He presented it to his general, the one wearing Kelly's flesh, who brought it to his slobbering beak to nip chunks from it.

Kelly went limp with death, the only mercy afforded to the young woman, before Ah-Puch went about opening her abdominal cavity to scatter her innards to the throng waiting to feast upon them. They came running up the steps to gather every bloody morsel of her insides, fighting over long cords of intestine. The king of the dead claimed his prize by lodging his thumbs in her nasal cavities while wrapping his massive hands about her skull then twisting it free from her delicate neck. The rest of her was rolled down the stairs to a waiting crowd with a seemingly endless hunger for fresh meat. Her head was placed upon a stake beside him before he turned back to those awaiting the same gory end. His cruelty brought him great amusement, and it had been ages since such celebrating had taken place in his lands of torment. He planned to revel in the bloody festivities before stepping back into the world of the living to gather more tributes to bring back to Xibalba.

CHAPTER NINE

Alissa limped along behind Wes who held the lantern out before them, inspecting the cavern top to bottom as they made their way forward. He had found an opening at the opposite side of the previous cavern and Alissa had nearly fallen through so they decided to follow it. It seemed like they had trekked through the darkness forever with their breathing the only sound filling their ears in the stifling blackness, until then a faint light could be seen in the distance.

"Do you see it?" His whispering startled her.

"Yes," she answered.

Alissa wanted nothing more than to run forward, to break through the stone walls around them to find the daylight and open air, but she knew better than to react hastily after her fall. Wes moved as quickly as he could with Alissa in tow, and the blue light grew in intensity. They found themselves standing in the entrance of a house-sized chamber. Its walls were adorned with torches burning with ghostly blue flame.

"I don't like this," Wes spoke.

"Look, on the other side is a doorway," Alissa said as her eyes beheld the rectangular hole on the opposite wall.

Cautiously they stepped into the chamber and its illumination encircled them like a pale halo. The lantern Wes held bathed them in yellow light, and both felt their anxiety building. Alissa gripped his shoulder as they kept on a slow course forward. The smell of the deep caves in which they had slunk through was like wet soil, yet the large chamber held a bitter, acidic stench. A high-pitched shriek above them rattled them into a panicked run. Wes yanked Alissa along by the rope as he fled for the exit, only to stop abruptly which caused her to tumble over onto the cave floor. Alissa lifted herself up as Wes began back-stepping. A handful of torches before them snuffed out as something very large passed over them, blocking their escape. The screech resounded again, only this time it was out in front of them. Alissa had yet to fully see the cause of Wes's terror, but she didn't question it either. He was rushing backwards, pushing her in the direction in which they came. It worried her that he didn't wish to turn his back on whatever it was skittering across the stone floor after them. Wes was knocked to the ground and as he swung the lantern in self-defense Alissa could see a monstrous flat head with pincher-like mandibles. Antennas as long as her arm whipped ferociously as Wes battered it back with the lantern. It had no true eyes that could be distinguished and it seemed to Alissa that the closer it got, the more the brightness of their lamp seemed to alarm the creature. The odor it emitted made the thin cave air noxious to breathe. Alissa pulled her shirt up over her nose and mouth before searching the ground to find a rock the size of her palm. She threw the stone with all of her strength against its head, which made it rear up revealing a segmented body carried upon hundreds of short, spiny legs. She pulled Wes up by his collar as the lantern was swiped from his hand. They ran for the doorway through which they had entered. Alissa pulled a torch from the wall as they were met by the utter darkness of the previous passage. The clacking of the pointed legs of the human-sized centipede drew closer as it cast the lantern aside in favor of the human prey. It pursued them, snapping its jaws, screeching hungrily as it hurried after them.

Wes gripped Alissa's shoulder as he urged her to move faster. Their legs nearly became entangled in the guide rope between them. Wes gathered it quickly to allow a faster retreat. Her lungs were in agony, and it worried her she might hyperventilate before they could escape the predator behind them.

"RUN!"

She didn't have the breath to answer him as she pushed her body to its limit. Alissa held the torch out ahead of her, its flame hardly cut the darkness engulfing them. She prayed she wouldn't fall into the mouth of the mountain again, her bloody chin stung in remembrance of how close she came to death. They ascended upon the black hole of a doorway, one they had passed not a half an hour before. Wes grabbed her by the hand, as he too would never forget her fall. He pressed them both flat against the rock wall as the creature burst through the entryway in their path, snapping its pincher mouth. Like its much smaller cousins dwelling in the world above, the beast was nearly blind, its heightened sense of smell was leading it onward in a frenzy to a small pool of blood left from Alissa's injury. It went tumbling into the massive pit, its shrieking echoed up from the hole as it fell reverberating down the cavern, followed by the overwhelming stench of its broken body as it made contact with the floor of jagged boulders decimating its armored frame.

****

The Lord of Death was then joined by the high-ranking demon kings who were previously among the crowd below, reveling in the freshly slaughtered human woman. They had countenances of twisted creatures, half-human and half-beast, adorned with feathers and bones. Their mouths slavered like hungry carnivores. Tyler's broken body was carried to the stone with his gut already split from his drop into the cave. The kings were brought elaborate seats from within the temple to sit upon while they dined. Ah-Puch plunged his arms into the dead man's abdominal cavity to gather gifts for his men. Each was granted a fistful of gore on which to feast voraciously, spreading their terrible countenances with blood. Dennis had his eyes closed when a keening screech halted the repast, silencing all those in attendance. It echoed loudly out of one of the many black voids dotting the cavern walls. The owl man adorned in the skin of Kelly signaled to his men who leaped into the air on their misshapen wings to soar over to the source of the din. A hand at his throat signaled that his turn upon the sacrificial stone had come.

****

The torch was hardly a source of light, yet it served to guide them back to where their lantern had been swiped from Wes's hands. Luckily it was still operational, but they were both aware the battery wouldn't last forever. They crossed the chamber in which the creature had attacked them to find the dark exit. Wes took the lead once more as they stepped into a narrow passageway. Its ceiling was so high it could not be seen by the lantern light. A cool wind blew down upon them as they journeyed onward and it made it easier to breathe, yet it caused them to feel oddly exposed for it was no earthly breeze. It was then Alissa knew the path they were following would only lead them back into the cavern of misery...Xibalba.

****

The din filled the passageway echoing from the stone walls. Wes pulled Alissa down to crouch at the cave's mouth. Her nightmare became reality when she stared out over the grey lands of death. The clatter grew louder, a flapping of wings followed by a shrill screeching voice speaking an indistinguishable command, and it sounded just above them in another of the myriad of cave entrances. Alissa looked to Wes. They both knew what hunted them. She stared back in despair at the black tunnels they had already fought through, unwilling to enter the bowels of the mountain again. He clenched her hand before motioning with his head before them. Their only escape was a long drop into a tangled, withered forest below them. Wes killed the lantern before looping his belt through its handle to secure it to him. Alissa followed as he lowered himself to suspend over a bed of thorny vines. The twisted jungle was lit by a faint green light reminiscent of fireflies. Her arms trembled as she hung there, judging the distance of the fall caused her to panic. She tried hoisting herself back up, yet her hands didn't have the strength.

"We have to let go," Wes whispered.

"NO!"

CHAPTER TEN

The shrieking from the depths of the cave alerted them that the Wayobs had discovered their trail and that the deformed creatures would be upon them soon. Wes released his grip, then went falling, disappearing into the barbed arms of the vines below. Alissa looked up at her shaking hands as a single downy feather drifted down to caress her cheek. A stench followed. Blood. The rope between them tugged her hands free, and she felt her stomach crawl up into her throat. Her brain vainly attempted to reconcile with the fact her body was about to impact the unknown when she halted midair. Alissa felt stabbing pain in her legs and abdomen. She opened her eyes to see she had been caught seconds before falling onto a bed of jagged stones. It felt like getting a hundred piercings all t once as the vines held her in their thorny grip. Wes hung beside her in much the same condition, a barb stuck into his lower cheek, a second had penetrated only an inch from his eye. For a moment, the two of them could only remain absolutely still, making the pain tolerable. Alissa moaned faintly as Wes tried to remove his right arm, and the vibration sweeping through the vines stung her wounds, yet she was aware they had to pull themselves free. He gritted his teeth as he slid the thorns slowly from his forearm; it was being wrapped in barbed wire. It left a line of warm blood where the vine was finally torn from him. It was only the beginning of a tedious process, each arm and leg had been punctured more times than he could count, plus there were those driven deeply into the flesh of his back and stomach leaving him to be an impaled marionette suspended above the forest floor.

"Once I'm free I'll help you," he said. "Just hold on."

Above them it grew black, blotting out the torch light, with swarming half men. Their cries caused Wes to hurriedly start yanking thorns free from his skin, tearing them out painfully. He braced himself as he brought a shaking hand up to dislodge the spikes from his cheek. Alissa watched tears run from his eyes as he grunted, biting his lip in an attempt to be as silent as possible. The thorns moved gradually as he pried them from his face. Alissa could see the quiet determination in his quavering arms as at last they came out. Wes released a heavy sigh as he turned his head to inspect those in his back. As he had liberated his arms and legs, the vines piercing his back and abdomen sagged, stretching his skin like a suspension performer. The scene reminded her of the depictions she had seen in history books of the Cheyenne sun dance rituals. The jolts of burning agony reminded Alissa her fate was the same as his. The thorns piercing the skin of Wes's back gave way beneath his weight dropping him to the rocky forest floor. He impacted with a short cry. Alissa looked upward to see if he had drawn the attention of the Wayobs above them. The creatures halted and she knew they would soon be found out. Frantically, she began yanking the thorns from her skin and some tore clean through leaving gaping wounds. Her flesh felt as if it had been set on fire and blood soaked through her shirt. Exhausted, Alissa hung for a moment by a row of spines gripping her by the fat of her lower back. Wes came to let her straddle his shoulders in the hopes it would ease her suffering.

"Try to break the vine. I'll pull them out," he said.

Alissa turned back to grip the vine weakly; she twisted it, bent it in two, tried tearing it apart and yet it wouldn't be destroyed. They should have known since it was strong enough to hold them it would be impossible to snap it with the strength of her hands alone.

The Wayobs fluttered down above the copse of thorny vines growing at the base of the cave walls, squawking wildly when they spotted the human still ensnared in the sharp arms of the hungry plants, yet they held cautiously back.

Alissa could feel the thorns in her skin pulsating as she bled over them. The plant appeared to be nothing more than a dormant mess of knotted vines, and yet it began to glow faintly as it supped upon the blood of the humans who fell into it. Wes kicked at the spiny arms of it as it came to life and sought to reclaim him. Alissa did the only thing she knew to do to help them escape. She reached back, gripped the throbbing vine, then tore it from her skin. It claimed large chunks of flesh yet she was finally free of it. Alissa tumbled from Wes's shoulders screaming.

"Run!"

He retreated, but turned around when he realized she wasn't at his side. Alissa's legs were tangled in the slow yet strong grip of the vines and she fought feebly as it tried to encompass her. The monsters above them watched from the withered tops of leafless trees, laughing like mockingbirds as she struggled for her life.

****

The corpse of the final human was dragged into the chambers within the pyramid then deposited in the darkness by the zombified old man. The lord made Professor Lipton a slave in reward for opening the gate to the land of the living. Dennis had been decapitated just to appease the crowds of raucous dead. Ah- Puch kept his head and body for further feasting with his men.

It had been centuries since the priestess shed her blood in the hopes of sealing the land of fear forever. She had been amongst the dark forests when a blue light beckoned her to look in the direction of the antechamber, where her bones still rested. The disc had been taken, breaking the seal. She walked as a shade in the realm of fear. She could have ascended to the world amongst the stars a lifetime before, as it was decreed by the gods upon the sacrifice of her own blood, yet she declined in favor of spending the afterlife wreaking havoc in the lands of Xibalba. She stalked with the eyes of night, able to see as a nocturnal hunter into total darkness. Amidst the bloody revelry at the temple's base she was able to slip into its gory inner chambers where she found Dennis's body. She knew he was being held aside to further the festivities in private where the lord and his demon kings would dine upon each piece of his body. She held her spectral fingers over his eyelids, in hopes of glimpsing his final hours alive. It was revealed to her the expedition, the finding of the disc painted Mayan Blue, and the horrors within the mountain. The priestess knew there was a young woman and a young man still alive, yet she wasn't sure if they had made it into Xibalba. The commotion she had heard echoing into the temple as the Wayobs were ordered to hunt gave her reason to believe they had. She was nothing more than a moving shadow as she hurried out of the temple seeking the owl men.

****

The sanguinary vines were steadily sinking thorns into Alissa's skin, feeding off of her blood and growing stronger only to turn to sink more barbs into her flesh. Wes picked up a stone, then threw it into the tangle of creepers, but got no response. A cord found its way around her neck causing him to rush into the arms of the plant in an attempt to pull Alissa free. Wes began yanking the barbs from her flesh only to find himself being tied up in them. Alissa screamed as a thorn was roughly pulled from the side of her neck and a stream of blood traced its way down her shoulder. The plant seemed to sense its meal was attempting escape so it began to tighten its grip on her legs. Wes found he was unable to break free of the vampiric vines, as their strength had multiplied with the sustenance of Alissa's blood. The Wayobs took flight with taunting hoots of victory. Wes looked to the trees as they came to life with tiny humanoid faces, hundreds of sets of small, dark eyes bearing witness to them being bled dry.

****

Ah-Puch received the message with a grin. He sat at the head of a long table, around it seated his wicked kings, who too were delighted with the thoughts of more human flesh to collect. He had adorned his seat with the severed head of Kelly whose blue eyes shown like prized sapphires.

They roved over the macabre feast that was about to commence. The wall behind the Lord of Death was fitted with wooden shelves, displaying a collection of hearts he had cut from some of the mighty warriors who found themselves cast into Xibalba. The pyramid had many levels, each housed trials and booby-traps made to inflict torment on those who were set free into them. It was a form of entertainment for the macabre kings. There were many who never left the land of fear, becoming the same twisted and cruel creatures that crowded around the temple begging for hunks of flesh. Even worse, they became the feast itself, with pieces reserved as gruesome trophies.

Dennis's naked corpse laid upon the table top, split from his ruined neck down to his scrotum, splayed open to exhibit a buffet of organs within him. The master of Xibalba motioned to one of his sovereigns, instructing him to go forth to gather the humans once they were weak enough, then set them free amongst the trials of the pyramid for entertainment. His liege arose, the winged demon of blood with the face of a bat, to do the bidding of Ah-Puch. The Master of Xibalba then summoned Dennis's spirit back into his body. He screamed silently, his head severed from his neck, watching in pure agony as the gory banquet began.

****

They looked like tiny skeletal men in the soft green light of the dead forest, but it wasn't until they began jumping from branch to branch that Wes could distinguish the shape of their hairy little bodies. He realized then they were spider monkeys only very frail, the markings in their white and black fur depicted skeletons. They began shrieking then leaping to the forest floor to scoop up stones to throw at the attacking vines. He didn't dare hope the miniature army could possibly free them, as even then he could feel himself losing consciousness as the thorns sunk deep into his flesh. A handful of them flew through the trees, skipping from limb to limb with grace until his eyes could see them no more. The others continued tossing rocks, coming closer to tease the vines into letting go of the humans they sought to consume. It was a two-pronged attack. The smaller unit returned as a group above their heads carrying a blue-flamed torch before slipping it into the hungry plant. It erupted into a mass of burning limbs, releasing Wes and Alissa as it swept over them in a wave, singeing their hair. He managed to drag her across the ground before falling over her as the thorny arms of his attacker whipped out wildly, slicing his side open as he beat her back to be certain her clothing would not catch fire. A prickly vine wrapped about his ankle in its last moments in an attempt to claim him once more, yet the fierce liberation force leaped upon it, tearing it free of Wes with their mouths and paws. The bloodthirsty plant hissed as it shriveled back becoming lifeless once more.

Wes sat up to cradle his companion against his chest, shocked the blue fire didn't burn them. Alissa was pale with blood loss. Her countless puncture wounds ran red; soaking into her clothes in splotches of deep crimson. The gash in her chin looked deep but had ceased its bleeding, leaving a hole marring her simple beauty. Her head lulled listlessly to the side as he placed his palm to her cold cheek. "Please wake up," he said quietly.

Tiny, white fingers swept over the back of his hand. Wes looked up to see they were surrounded by the spider monkeys, and in their big, dark eyes he thought he could see concern. There sounded a faint whistle and they parted as a rippling shadow walked among them, a figure of complete darkness blotted out the phosphorescent glow of the forest floor. A hollow, feminine voice spoke to him in a language he could not decipher. Though he understood not a word spoken, he felt comfort radiating from the entity. The silhouette of a hand passed over Alissa's face, pausing for a moment over her eyes; they began to flutter as the ancient one whispered healing prayers. Wes wondered if she was no other than the priestess who sacrificed her own blood to seal the caverns.

A piercing shriek ricocheted from the stone walls entombing them and causing the monkeys to flee to the tree tops. Alissa awoke to the hurried confusion of Wes throwing her over his shoulder and then running with her through the reaching limbs of the dead forest.

CHAPTER ELEVEN

He had come to gather the humans before they perished from exsanguination. The thirsty vines did not obey the Wayob yet they did the Blood King. He swooped over them and saw they had been set aflame, as blue fire was hungrily consuming their empty arms. He screeched in defeat, the Lord of the Dead would not be pleased if he did not return with the entertainment. A legion of the skeleton monkeys screamed as they retreated into the heart of the barren jungle. Amidst the dead trees he spied a human man with a woman slung over his shoulder. He brought himself down to the forest floor, sniffing the air for blood, tasting it upon his tongue. It had been far too long since his lord hunted the monkey kind within the jungle of Xibalba. About his neck hung a conch shell, and he brought it to his pursed lips then blew it. It bellowed across the forest of death, sounding the call of the hunt.

****

Wes felt, as well as heard, the conch shell horn's blast as it rattled through his weakened body. He could feel his strength waning, his back ached then his knees began to wobble. Alissa was slung over his shoulder as he fought to keep up with their liberators. The nimble, skeleton-coated monkeys were leaping and swinging through the limbs of the dead trees while the shadow woman darted in and out of sight. The darkness of Xibalba was only broken by the dim illumination of the forest floor, like a glow in the dark moss it sprouted in thick patches casting soft, green light. The cavern walls were fitted with the undying azure flames, yet the surroundings were mostly black, like being caught in constant night. Terror filled Wes as the horn called once more, and he knew it would only be meant to attract the attention of the walking corpse with an Owl's head, the Lord of Death.

"I can walk," Alissa said.

The sound of her voice startled him from his thoughts, and his mind began recalling everything he knew of the land of fear. Everything he had read of the Mayan underworld had depicted the many trials within Xibalba along with the merciless lords ruling over it. Wes eased her onto her feet before taking her arm to drag her into retreat once more. He pulled her along behind him as he desperately searched for the simian shadows amongst the trees. They had disappeared into a copse of pale-barked trunks. Alissa stumbled beside him as he rushed them onward. She too had heard the call of the hunt, and the terror it instilled in Wes was visible. Alissa wished then they were still hidden in the suffocating inner passageways of the mountain. She felt so vulnerable and as if they were being stalked. She shuddered to think of what would be done with them once they were found, which she thought might be a certainty.

They fought through the tangled limbs of small trees reaching out to claw strips of flesh from their arms. Alissa shivered recalling already being nearly eaten, and she lashed out at the branches only to feel them snapping, their brittle shards left clinging to her shirt like the fingernails of corpses. The tiny skeletons awaited them beyond the obstacles.

"What are they?" Alissa asked.

"They were supposed to represent human souls of earth. The Lord of Death would hunt them here to cause people to die in our world."

"How did this all come to be here?" she asked.

"The doors told of their journey, being followed by death. They settled here and so did he," Wes answered. "There are doors to Xibalba in many places. It's a separate world all together, and any portal you enter, be it here or thousands of miles away, you'll find yourself in these lands."

"Is there a way out?" Alissa asked as they became surrounded by the skeleton-coated tribe. "We saw the chamber with the door get consumed with those vines, but is there another way?"

Wes shook his head in confusion. "I can't say for certain. I could only decipher that the priestess's blood and the disc were what kept the doorway closed. Professor Lipton broke that seal."

"You couldn't read any more than that?"

"I'm not the expert. He's fuckin' dead, remember?" Wes answered.

"Is this Hell? Are we in Hell?" she whispered.

He sat contemplating her question before answering.

"We're in the land of the dead..."

The monkeys scattered as the conch shell trumpeted once more. An arrow sailed through the impossible tangle of branches, pinning one of them through its fragile chest against a tree trunk. It screeched, then danced wildly upon the shaft in which it was impaled. Alissa took off running through the trees with Wes right behind her, arrows flying through the air around them, their propulsion stopped abruptly as they landed in the trees and the phosphorescent moss. Her heart raced as she dodged trees to avoid being slowed down. Wes's heavy breaths were right behind her, she could tell he was already winded after attempting to carry her over his shoulder. A dull *thunk* followed by a short gasp and a clatter caused her to look behind. She stopped at the sight of Wes lying on his stomach. The lantern was lying beside him, and an arrow was lodged deeply in his right side. Alissa gripped his hand, then dragged him up onto his feet.

"Let's go!" she cried.

"Can't...breathe," he gasped.

She wrapped his left arm around her then started to help him along. A trumpeting blast behind them indicated their hunter was upon them.

****

The blood gatherer was joined by the Wayob. Their leader still wore the prized skin of the woman. Flight was not an option amongst the trees so the demon king sent a handful of the owl men up to flutter above the bare branches while the rest hunted on foot. They brought with them the finest of hunting bows, bestowed upon them by Ah-Puch at the blood bringer's conch signal. A hunt hadn't been orchestrated in the dead jungle for a time unnumbered, and so the skeleton tribe wasgrowing far too strong. They now had drawn the attention of the lords of death by freeing the humans and the toll for their interference would be costly.

Within a stand of white barked trees, the humans were spotted from above. The Wayobs quietly descended to report to their master. He brought the conch shell up to his mouth then let it ricochet through the trees a final time. It sent the small ones fleeing wildly through the trees, abandoning the humans who could not move as quickly or nimbly. Blood Bringer brought his bow up, nocked an arrow, and then freed it to pierce the soft fur of a skeleton coat. Its cries of death could be heard throughout the barren forest. The humans bounded through the trees and the hunters pursued them intently, unwilling to let them escape into the darkest heart of the wood. They broke through the stand of white trees to see their prey desperately seeking an escape. The Wayobs loosed their arrows, and they went singing by their human targets. Blood Bringer could taste their fear, and it hung in the air with the smell of their sweat and blood. He nocked his second arrow, held his breath while aiming, then released it as he did the taught bow string. It sailed straight, cutting the air in two, and it found its mark. The human dropped onto his stomach, but his companion helped him to his feet before assisting him to hobble along. The hunters slowed their pace, since it was now becoming entertaining to let them struggle on. The demon king brought the conch to his lips to signal their end.

****

"Let's go!" Alissa said.

"Can't..." Wes shook his head. "I'm already dead...we're dead."

His sobs were breathless, silent heaving. The arrow had pierced his side and gone through his body, its head thrusted through his skin and t-shirt leaving him soaked in blood. His face was going white, stealing the color from his lips, and the severity of his condition wrenched her heart.

"We have to keep going," Alissa pleaded.

Wes's face had grown ashen; he too knew how grave his situation was. He released her. "Run while you can. They are coming."

His sentence was punctuated by a second arrow finding its mark in his back. He lurched forward, as his breath was stolen from him.

"I can't leave you here."

"You'll never make it far carrying me," he gasped.

She knew he spoke the grim truth.

"Go!" he urged her as blood trickled from the corner of his mouth.

Cries of excitement were far too close. Wes nodded his head, "Go."

Alissa took his pack then ran with all of her strength, with the terror having already numbed her to the pain of clawing branches. She no longer felt her heart was seizing up or her lungs were burning with over exertion. She ran on phantom limbs, and for a moment it felt as if she were floating.

Behind her she could hear Wes screaming, agonizing cries climbing to the tops of the dead trees. Alissa wept as she ran, her eyes blurred with salty tears. She was alone in the land of fear, the kingdom of the dead stretched out before her to swallow her alive. Her foot caught the root of a tree protruding up out of the ground like the hand of a soul refusing death's lonesome sentence of isolation below the soil. Her vision tumbled along with her body as she was sent rolling down a steep bed ending in a warm, dark river. Alissa was forced below the current, and a moment of confused screaming rewarded her with a mouthful of a liquid, leaving her mouth tasting like she had sucked on a handful of pennies. Alissa surfaced, choking up mouthfuls of stomach bile. Her nose was filled with the scent of blood.

She rode the waves, trying to regain control of her body before she was drowned completely. A screeching above her told Alissa she had been spotted by one of the owl men. She held her breath, allowed herself to be pulled beneath the rolling currents and tossed against the rocks like jagged teeth set amongst the tumbling water.

****

The Wayob dressed in Kelly's skin took flight at Blood Bringer's command. His master had already claimed the other human with two arrows to his back. The other hunters had gathered around him, each taking turns to push the arrow slowly further through the wound in his side. The Demon King got the final laugh by placing his calloused foot against the human's back before yanking the arrow free. It caused the prey to scream like an animal in the throes of death. The Wayobs danced about, delighting in the torment they were inflicting yet the hunt wasn't complete so the master sent his best man to search for the pale-skinned woman who got away. His vision was that of a nocturnal predator, zeroing in on her as she ran. He watched her stumble, then roll down the steep bank of the blood river before splashing into its crimson currents. She

169

popped back up, coughing and gagging. The Owl man kept his golden eyes on her as she bobbed within the rushing waters, her body tumbled as she was tossed against the black rocks protruding from the river bottom. The girl was lost amongst the undercurrents. He sought for her for a time, knowing no human could withstand being submerged so long and live. He flew away to report to Blood Bringer that the river had claimed her. Their next task would be to dredge her up.

****

Alissa fought to hold her breath, but her lungs had reached their limit. The river flowed rapidly around her, forcing her down, slamming her against stones. Her body was pushed beneath the submerged boughs of a fallen tree and its branches tore her skin while her hair wound tightly around them. Alissa's eyes stung when she opened them to the murky, red liquid. She yanked at her hair, pulling a handful of it from her own scalp in a frantic attempt to free herself. Her nostrils burned, the river would soon invade her body as her natural reaction to breathe would take place. She was aware once she started to drown it would be nearly impossible in her weakened state to stop it. In defeat she screamed, nothing but a muffled whimper traveled to the surface wrapped in a crimson bubble. Tiny hands gripped her cheeks as Alissa flung a hand out at shadows entering the water. Her wrist locked in a firm grip yanking her hand back as something was pressed against her mouth. Alissa still struggled feebly before she realized the skeleton coat was attempting to force air into her lungs. She settled back before accepting the meager yet life-giving breaths gratefully. Panic still surged through Alissa, as her body was trapped beneath the crushing red water, and her chest felt as if it might cave in at any minute from the weight of it pressing her down. The skeleton coats went to work, linking together to form a chain to free Alissa's hair from its entanglement. They usually stayed clear of the rushing river, as it had claimed many of them in the past. She felt her legs being assisted back out from under the rotten tree branches seeking to restrain her until the blood river passed through her body just as it did between its twisted boughs. Her body was freed, yet Alissa didn't have the strength to swim against the currents. The tiny warriors caught her by the arms, an army of them working together to save her as they clung desperately to fallen trees and rocks. Alissa was drug up onto the river bed, then she crawled beneath low-hanging branches filled with dead leaves. Above her spoke softly a feminine voice soothing her into relaxation. Her back was cushioned by a bed of phosphorescent moss, and its glow calmed her as she breathed deeply the air of Xibalba.

CHAPTER TWELVE

Wes was hogtied to a long, limbless branch then born up between the shoulders of the Blood King and the owl men. The hunters had stripped him of his clothing down to his boxers before roughly tying his wrists and ankles to the splintered shaft of wood. They bounced him as they carried him in a ceremonious dance of victory. He hung listlessly; his pain was so overwhelming he couldn't scream. His wrists felt as if they would surely separate from their sockets each time he was jostled. The owl men who weren't tasked with bearing the load of flesh were tauntingly hopping about, prodding him with the tips of their arrows. The hunting party found their way to the long stone road leading to the temple. Wes could see vaguely without his glasses lines of blue- flamed torches running alongside them as they continued their hymns of triumph. He knew his final destination would be the top of the pyramid where death would surely be waiting.

****

The priestess sat guard over the girl while she rested. The skeleton tribe had reported to her the hunters had left the forest since the young man had become their trophy. They carried to her the lantern the young man had lost in his capture and managed to pull the pack free from the girl's back hoping she could rest better. Shadow Priestess had been a shade so long--for centuries roaming the reaches of Xibalba to corners of the lands that even the Lord of Death himself hadn't seen, with her only companions being the small tribesmen of the skeleton coats. Ah-Puch now controlled the antechamber door since the seal had been broken. The priestess had nothing left to sacrifice anymore as she was merely a specter, but she did know of a way the girl may be able to return to the above world of the living.

When Alissa opened her eyes and realized she still lay upon the bank of a river she was positive flowed blood instead of water, she nearly broke down. She sat up at a soft whistling. Though Alissa had lost her glasses within the pit in the caverns she could still see decently. The shadow woman sat not far away, Alissa could discern her petite shape outlined atop the glowing moss. Alissa knew this shade who had summoned the tribe of skeleton coats to her rescue must have been a figure of great importance in her lifetime. A priestess or a queen or perhaps both. She stood up after a moment and motioned for Alissa to take the lantern and follow her.

****

Ah-Puch sat atop the great pyramid, watching as Blood Bringer returned from the hunt. His other lieges stood at the top of the steep stone stair, each of them experts in their own forms of torture, every one of them adorned in feathers and bone. They awaited the arrival of the new flesh, offering to drain him of every drop of his precious blood amidst the trials within the temple.

Wes felt the warmth of his own body escaping him with every drop off his blood that seeped from the deep holes on his side and back, leaving a dark trail upon the cracked roadway, and he began to tremble violently. His arms and legs ached at the sockets. He prayed shock would end his life as nausea tore its way through his gut. He vomited a single, hot mouthful of bile, and it came back down in his face adding to his humiliation and torture. One of his captors squawked mockingly, and then kicked him in his injured side sending a shock of blinding pain up his spine. His vision blurred and he felt himself slipping away. A screeching ahead of them brought back the terrifying remembrance of the other entities dwelling in the lands of fear--those that would certainly gather at the foot of the pyramid as hungry as vultures to pick his splintered bones clean.

****

The skeleton coat leaped upon the crumbling stone roof of a small tomb-like building. She dropped down low to slink to the highest point of the rubble. She had been sent on a reconnaissance mission by the Shadow Priestess. The darkness shrouded her yet her white markings were easily distinguishable especially by the keen eyes of the Wayobs. It was no secret to where the human would be taken yet the priestess wished to know of his physical condition. The train of deformed predators could be seen approaching, bathed in pale, blue light; the human was customarily tied to a fallen limb of a white barked ghost tree. The skeleton coat lay her belly flat down upon the frigid stone, barely summoning the courage to peek over the edge at those passing beneath her. She would have guessed the human to be dead if it weren't for him coughing up vomit. The priestess had to be made aware of the prisoner's dire condition, as her plan depended upon it. The skeleton coat watched them pass before retreating back to her home in the dead forest before the other insidious inhabitants of Xibalba could catch her scent.

****

Alissa trailed behind the shadow woman nimbly making her way through the tightly woven brush. She held the lantern, yet she left it cold and dark as they traversed the black heart of the wood. They didn't speak the same language so Alissa quickly grew accustomed to the priestess's whistling or the snap of her fingers as a signal. There were times she lost sight of the silhouette walking in front of her, such as in areas lacking the incandescent undergrowth where the priestess became lost in the darkness. Alissa was exhausted, and her body's natural clock had become disoriented by the perpetual night around her. The shadow woman halted at the tree line; before them stretched a glimmering meadow. Alissa heard a soft whisper at her ear, stopping her from leaving the shelter of the forest. The priestess stood behind her before bringing her spectral hand up over the girl's eyes, imparting a vision to her of a small river splitting the lands in two. Alissa knew by the way the shadow woman spoke to her that the current river was one she should not fall into.

As they approached the stream Alissa was struck by its nauseating stench, like a septic wound. She hadn't smelled anything that even came close to it, not even her time working at a nursing home changing adult diapers could match it. The shadow turned back to her, then demonstrated to Alissa to cover her mouth and nose with her hand. The scent became palpable even through clamped nostrils, eliciting bouts of heaving on Alissa's part. The rocky shore looked as if it was slick with yellow mucous. The river itself moved slowly, caught within its flow floated a bloated corpse of a skeleton coat, its skin slid from its corpse like a greasy peel. The currents about it crawled over its flesh, eating it away, and in the short time it took to float by, Alissa watched as it was nearly consumed. She understood then that the stream reeking of infection, like currents of pus, would kill her nearly instantly if she fell into it. Her clothes were still stained from the blood that nearly drowned her within its coppery tides, so she stepped away. The silhouette urged her onward, whistling as she showed Alissa the way across. There was a fallen tree that spanned most of the river before it ended at a single stone, large enough to stand upon, but also large enough to miss completely. Alissa shook her head.

"I can't make it," she said.

She watched as the silhouette walked slowly out across the log. The priestess took a moment to calculate her next leap before skillfully jumping out onto the stone just long enough to gain her footing, then bounded for the opposite bank. She hurriedly exited the stones just beyond the reach of the milky, yellow river. Alissa paced the river bed anxiously, she couldn't turn back, but she wasn't sure she could make it to the other side. The priestess did not fear the stinking currents since she was already dead. Alissa allowed her courage to build for a moment before proceeding. She stepped onto the fallen tree knowing there was no other option, and she felt it swaying beneath her feet. Alissa shuffled along and inched out farther, and the edge was far too close as she tossed the lantern over to the other bank. The river's stink seemed to swallow her up in its foul aroma; the compulsion to throw up gripped her stomach in a tight knot. When she looked to the stone to which she was supposed to jump she hesitated. It looked so much smaller from her new viewpoint. Insecurity rocked her, she stepped backwards. The log dipped with the transference of her body weight, and nearly tossed her off balance. She released her mouth and nose to use both arms to regain her stability. She was struck with the noxious vapors of the putrid river below and its smell of decay...of death. From the other side came chanting, though she did not know the words Alissa could feel it strengthening her, fortifying her will to survive. Alissa straightened her back, took two quick steps forward, then leaped to the small stone. She refused to let her eyes see the yellow stream or let its smell sway her again, and she leaped with all of herstrength, pushing herself forward with a powerful stride. She landed on the far shore where the priestess waited with a cry of victory. Alissa rejoiced in her crossing, yet she didn't know the trials beyond that point were far worse than any she had already encountered in the lands of fear.

****

Wes opened his eyes to see he was still hanging from the ghost tree limb. A crowd of walking corpses had gathered about the proud hunting party bearing putrid smiles with dried out long-receded lips licked by ravenous violet tongues. The skin left clinging to their bones was pale indigo where Mayan Blue had lasted for centuries. The bat-faced creature was obviously in charge shrieking before kicking a talon-tipped foot out at them; causing the horde to fall back in terror. They were dead, yet they feared him, and it made Wes tremble to think that in this place even after death his suffering would not end. He felt himself hanging at an angle as the Blood Demon began ascending the steps of the pyramid temple. The crowd cheered as they began the climb; soft blue torch light illuminated their way up the bloodstained stairs. Wes knew the owl-headed master would be at the top to greet him, though it delighted the macabre throng when he cried out not knowing what more he could possibly do.

Blood Gatherer was greeted by his demon brethren as they reached the summit of the pyramid. They came to inspect his prize of the hunt; a pale-skinned human bleeding from an arrow wound in his side. The bow shot had produced a through and through set of holes in the flesh of the prey, and by their placement it was clear internal bleeding was a certainty. Wes was tossed to the stone floor roughly so the ghoul kings could exchange cordial formalities. Their grotesque faces leered down at him as they spoke in guttural voices, each one a twisted coupling of man and beast, more horrid than anything he had ever witnessed in his most twisted of nightmares. Remembering he was only clothed in his boxers left him feeling all the more vulnerable. He would have wished for death yet the group of hungry corpses told him the end of his life would not equal release.

CHAPTER THIRTEEN

The shadow woman proceeded in a much more cautious manner on the other side of the diseased river. Alissa could feel her apprehension and it made her own anxiety multiply. There was also much less moss casting light, therefore the priestess motioned to the lantern Alissa gripped in her sweaty palm. She pressed the button, nearly blinding her with the bright orb of yellow light. It made her nervous to think she could now be spotted from a great distance by the light source she held, but there was no other means for her to find her way in the lands beyond the stinking river's shore.

Alissa crept along behind the feminine silhouette guiding her. Before them stretched a seemingly endless forest of thin-trunked trees. She kept her breathing shallow as if drawing her lungs full could somehow give her away to the creatures who might seek to harm her. Her confidence was sorely diminished because the priestess was treading with great caution. There were keening, high-pitched voices caught in the wind filling the wood, and its source could not be determined for it seemed to dance about them from all sides. Alissa spun, staring deep into the darkness of the wood only to see more of the skeletal trees. They were stark white and fragile like fleshless finger bones protruding from the black soil of Xibalba. For the first time since stepping beyond the crumbling stone doors Alissa felt a breeze on her skin, one so cold she would have guessed the onset of winter had found them. Shadow Priestess stepped into the yellow circle of light then passed her hand over Alissa's eyes, and granted her a vision of creature. The monster cowered in the presence of light and she held the lantern over them encircling them in its warm yellow glow. This image caused Alissa to panic, and she felt the fear of her companion beside of her, terror holding her still. She didn't dare breathe, let alone run. The keening became a very distinct screaming, a cry of someone who had been deeply betrayed. Just beyond the touch of the lantern light materialized the entity of what appeared to be a woman, yet her scalp had been completely shorn of its hair, she had deep empty holes for eyes, and a mouth of jagged black teeth. Alissa resisted the urge to shriek. The wailing continued as the spirit seemed to search for them though the lantern's orb kept it at bay. It moved in fast halting motions as it tasted the air with a long, forked tongue. Alissa held her breath as it came just beyond the lantern's light to scream, and a piercing cry caused her body to grow cold and tremble. She realized then as she stared directly at its face just how reptilian it appeared as it swiped a clawed hand at the intruders hiding within the glowing yellow bubble.

A sound akin to thunder boomed in the distance followed by a rumbling that shook the forest earth, and the creature turned her scaly head in its direction. The reptilian woman was silenced by a second resounding bang echoing amongst the thin trees. The hunter dashed away back into the cold, dark distance. Alissa released her breath.

"Nagual" was whispered in her ear, and though Alissa did not understand the word itself she knew the shadow woman was imparting the beast's name to her.

They stood for a long while, silently searching their surroundings. Once the priestess was satisfied it was safe to proceed, she whistled softly to Alissa then they continued their cautious journey through the deepest parts of the forest.

****

Wes was forced upon his feet only to feel his head spinning as if he would faint. The pain was intense, his blood loss too great, and he crumpled to the stone floor. The lord of death, Ah-Puch, grabbed a fistful of Wes's dark hair then lifted him up off of the ground. Wes hung face-to-face with the owl-headed underworld god; the stench emanating from him was like an opened grave. Ah-Puch lifted his pointer finger, held it between their faces as it began to glow white hot like smoldering embers. Wes opened his mouth to scream only to have his cries choked back within his throat as his breath was instantly stolen when the master of fear ran his fiery finger into the open arrow wound. Wes could smell his flesh cauterizing as unimaginable torment burned inside of him. The Lord of Death withdrew his finger only to repeat the procedure with the hole in Wes's back before letting him fall back onto the cold stone floor.

Bone King was given the task of restraining the young man until Ah-Puch felt he was ready to be put through the trials. He was no more than a skeleton draped in leathered hide with a bulbous swollen gut, and though he was small in stature, he bore unearthly strength. Wes knew even in his best shape he would not be able to break free of the grip of the skeletal creature that dragged him along by the ankles.

The interior of the pyramid was quite dark, a few torches hung from the walls yet they couldn't shine through the utterly black atmosphere. Wes was hauled past the dining hall where he caught a glimpse of Dennis's corpse split open upon a table laden with goblets and dishes filled with bloody entrails. A throne made of yellowed bones sat at the head of the table, impaled upon the headrest was a fleshless skull with blue eyes. It sickened him to think of the once-powerful young man who had his entire life ahead of him; a life of privilege no doubt, reduced to a pile of cannibalized leftovers. Wes desperately gripped the edge of the doorway as they went by, only to be kicked in the gut until he laid submissively limp once more, horrified as Dennis's mouth opened in a soundless cry and a tear slid down his pallid cheek.

****

The priestess had ventured through the dead forest before, but when she learned what dwelled in its darkest half she vowed never to return. She knew in the lands of fear true death and release did not exist, only unending torment, and that there were those who delighted in doling it out. One of those lived in a hovel not far from where they now tread. She was the forsaken daughter of Blood King. Blood maiden was only one of her monikers yet it suited her well. To the shadow woman's knowledge there was a hidden exit, a hole big enough for the girl to squeeze through at the bottom of a sink hole...if she could survive the journey through Blood Maiden's realm.

The Nagual had not been sighted again, yet her vicious calls had rung out several more times as they trudged silently along. The lantern that surrounded them in warm light was both a blessing and a curse, for Shadow Priestess feared they would be spotted by the keen eyes of the mistress of the forest. The girl walking beside her couldn't hide among the shadows of the trees or become invisible in the black voids of the caverns as the ancient spirit woman could do. The miniature sun Alissa held in her hand was her only protection against the Nagual, which was born of darkness and feared its purifying rays more than anything. The other creatures of Xibalba weren't so easily frightened; the Blood Maiden would laugh at the meager defense. The priestess had another mission beyond securing the girl's exit, and it would lead her to parlay with the skeleton coats before returning to the temple to seek the captured young man. She only prayed he could hold on until she found him.

Alissa was whistled to a stop before the silhouette beside her bent down looking at the soil. It had changed; only feet before it had been soft and black, now it was powdery gray like walking in ashes. The priestess stood, hovered her shadowy hand over Alissa's eyes, and showed her a vision of her own self. The beautiful priestess in her mind held her hand out in front of her in a motion that told Alissa to stay where she was as the priestess exited the safety of the light encompassing them. The silhouette became camouflaged by the shadows of the foliage; she could only discern when she passed over an occasional patch of moss or in front of a ghost tree.

Shadow Priestess concentrated on each step she took, recalling her first time encountering the Blood Maiden. Even as a spirit she barely escaped. The Blood Maiden fed upon energy and she nearly devoured the priestess who managed to flee while the mistress of the forest was distracted by the Wayobs bringing messages from Blood Bringer, her father. Since that meeting she normally avoided that part of the forest, but this circumstance was much different, for the pathway to the hidden exit began just beyond the Maiden's lair and behind a waterfall of frigid water. Unless they wanted to go back and risk a journey through the dead city, which would be suicide to the human, this was the best way. The rushing of the falls could be heard in the distance, signaling to the priestess that the maiden's dwelling was very close. The mistress was a trickster who caused animals and spirits to roam aimlessly, never finding their way out of the forest. A hunter just as her father, she took great pleasure in stalking and killing. Centuries of doing so had taught her the vilest ways of inflicting death. It was oddly calm, a fact that did not evade the shadow priestess's senses. She passed a twisted mass of thorny vines when she heard the sobs of a young woman.

****

The stone chamber was filled with incense smoke so thick Wes could hardly see. Among the billowing clouds he distinguished a figure hunched over a large three- legged stone pot. A headdress of feathers fell down the man's back, and his skin glistened with sweat along his bony back as he mixed a concoction within the massive bowl. Wes knew this man must be a priest of great importance or at least the spirit of one. Bone Demon had left him lying on the floor to be buried in smoke as the priest entity worked feverishly over the pot.

The priest turned to face the captive, with his fingers stained a deep blue. The specter's face was nothing but bone, a skull with blackened teeth. His skin hung loose from the bones of his emaciated body. He took up a small stone vessel then collected some of his work within it. Wes was familiar with such a ceremonious act and its significance. He would be painted Mayan Blue to represent that he was now a sacrifice of flesh and blood. Wes's body trembled as he was anointed with the pigment, which was still warm from being melted with the heat of the incense. It clung to his body like mud, masking his face with an indigo crust. The stink of rot hung about the priest, and it wafted into Wes's nostrils just below the smoky essence of the Mayan Blue paint. The priest's nasal cavity was filled with long-decayed tissue spider-webbing together in thin strands. His eyes were still present in his skull yet they were clouded with the presence of death. His long fingers worked their way over Wes's chest then down his abdomen, and he hesitated at the cauterized wound. Wes stared into the shaman's face, watched as a maggot surfaced hungrily within one of his eye sockets squirming its way over his milky iris. It dangled itself from the receded eyelid of the specter-made flesh, ravenously seeking fresh meat, and then dropped down onto Wes's stomach. He flinched yet the priest held him to the floor as the maggot inched towards his injury. Wes screamed as he attempted to yank his arms free, rocking his hips in desperation, trying to knock the flesh-eating worm off of him. The priest straddled Wes while pinning his arms down, watching the maggot creep closer to its new home within the young man's body. Wes screamed as it squirmed into his flesh then began burrowing feverishly downward to hide inside of the wound that had begun to grow infected. It twitched within him as his cries echoed from the stone walls, filling the temple with the depths of his desperation and fear.

CHAPTER FOURTEEN

Alissa trembled as she awaited the shadow's return. She couldn't help but feel the lantern she held in her quaking hand was nothing more than a beacon to the hungry beasts within the dead jungle. When the sobbing started in the distance it shook her, filled her with such a desperate need to flee, and she took off running. Alissa reminded herself she was instructed to stay where she was, yet the crying soon turned to terrible laughter, a cackling that sent her heart into her throat and her legs carrying her away before she could think rationally. She ran blindly in the dark forest, the lantern swinging before her face. Alissa kept her eyes squinted, frantically searching for the silhouette who had guided her into the dangerous wood. She still didn't know the reasoning for entering such a place. She just hoped the shadow woman was leading her to a place of safety. Her feet were swept out from under her, the dark forest spun around her as the lantern tumbled from her hand, breaking against the black stones of the jungle floor. The Nagual crawled upon her, clawing at Alissa's chest, snapping her vicious maw within inches of her prey's face. Alissa fought back, punching wildly, her fists contacting the leathery skull of the reptilian creature. It seized her by the wrist, driving its long, needle-like teeth into the soft flesh of her arm. Alissa used the butt of her palm to thrust upward in a quick jab to her attacker's throat. It released her arm, then rolled away to scurry up the side of a tree to recover from the blow. Alissa could barely make out its silhouette as it ascended the tree, yet she knew that it was preparing to leap upon her, and she turned to flee only to run directly into a tangled thorn vine. It gripped her legs, taking her to the ground, but the more she kicked it seemed the more she became tied up in them. Alissa could hear the hunter hiss then its claws digging into the soil as it jumped down to claim its meal. Its hot breath was soon at the back of her neck; the puncture wounds in her arm burned and bled, and she readied herself to feel those same teeth severing her spine.

A sorrowful crying caused the Nagual to jump nervously, and it retreated without protest into the darkness engulfing them. Alissa lay face down in the dirt and rocks, terrified to see the source of the weeping. The hair rose on her neck as she felt a presence leering over her. Once more the sobbing turned to lilting giggles, the laughter of a lunatic. Alissa felt fingers tousle her hair, softly toying with her dirty brown locks. The playfulness was tinged with violence for soon an entire hand was knotted in her tresses, and it wrenched her head back. A face edged into view slowly, a visage with dark eyes, caked with grey soot. The woman smiled, yet Alissa knew it held no kindness, and it reminded her more of a shark who had tasted blood in the water. Alissa was yanked painfully from the vines holding her before being taken by the hand. the gray-faced woman struck her with such fear she did not resist being led. Darkness surrounded them and she had no idea if the shadow woman was even aware of her capture.

****

His entire body was smothered in Mayan Blue paint before he was forced to get up and walk, to obediently follow behind Bone King into the labyrinth of trials within the temple. Wes's stomach lurched up into his throat and he turned aside to empty it upon the floor of the temple

195

passages. Bone King cackled then slapped Wes across the back of his head. The underworld demon was now adorned in a chest plate made of bones. A yellowed ribcage hung over his chest, finger bones hung from his hair while his face was masked in the remnants of a skull that had been cut in two from top to bottom. His arms were bare, but painted with red and white symbols and it was the same for his legs. Ah-Puch, along with a handful of his other lieges, awaited them at the opening of a great chamber in the bowels of the pyramid. They were specters wearing bodies of decay, leaking pus, and had skulls grinning with faces tight with rictus. A short-statured demon lord bore skin riddled with seeping lesions. Wes could smell the plague lord's fetid wounds from a good distance causing his nausea to multiply.

Ah-Puch ordered the human to be brought forth and the others cheered excitedly. Wes was pushed forward by the emaciated Bone King, bringer of famine, to face the owl-headed Lord of Death. His children, the Wayob, had been sent out again searching for the young woman's corpse. They would certainly enjoy dining upon her blood-sodden meat. The King of Xibalba eyed the sacrifice, adorned with the traditional blue paint, and he nodded with satisfaction.

Wes was forced through the stone doorway into a room of utter darkness, with not a single torch hung upon the walls. He was completely blind, and as he shuffled his feet and felt his way along, a low, rasping growl echoed behind him. Wes knew the trials within the temples were meant to be painful, humiliating, and also very deadly, and there was no time for error for it would cost him what was left of his life to bring them pleasure.

Blood Bringer toyed with the sacrifice to add to the entertainment as the kings of fear watched with the eyes of nocturnal hunters. He observed as the human inched closer to the first obstacle, as Blood King could have easily taken Wes's life at any moment yet he refrained just to watch the human pass through the pit of teeth.

****

Shadow Priestess knew she was too late to keep the girl safe when she no longer could locate the yellow orb of light in the distance. The Nagual sulked in the top of a tree as she snuck beneath it. The shattered lantern served as a starting point for her search yet she knew where Alissa would be found, she would be restrained within a small adobe house covered in soot and reeking of death.

Alissa was bound to a tall, wooden stake driven into the gravel floor of the sorceress's hovel. Her wrists were tied with a length of dead, thorny vine that bit into her skin almost as deep as the teeth of the Nagual. The girl was terrified yet stricken dumb by the black eyes of the blood maiden who now danced before her with the corpses of skeleton-coated monkeys tied up in the same barbed vines. The enchantress used them like tiny marionettes to act out morbid dramas of passion and murder. One moment she wept, then the next she laughed heartily while their flesh fell away to expose their delicate bones.

Shadow Priestess followed the sound of falling water for she recalled its rushing had awakened her the first time she found herself a victim of the Blood Maiden. She knew better now than to make eye contact with the ash-laden necromancer. The Nagual served as a reluctant watch dog to the sorceress, like an abused pet it slunk through the forest in hopes of being thrown the bones of its mistress's victims. It lay across a tree branch hanging out over the thatched roof of the maiden's dwelling place waiting for scraps of gristle to be cut from the human's body. In reality it was once a magic wielder itself, yet much less powerful than Blood Maiden, so in death it became her servant. The sorceress whistled to call for the Nagual. Shadow Priestess watched it climb into Blood Maiden's window. She grew nervous with the passing moments, knowing both creatures enjoyed eating flesh.

The reptile woman came in through the open hole in the wall, hissing at her master in annoyance. Blood Maiden bid the creature to sit before her new guest and the monster obeyed knowing she would be used as a conduit to speak with the loosened spirits of Xibalba. Her reward would be great for such a service as it always had been. The Blood Maiden thrived on devouring the sorrows and fears of her victims as well as their blood. An elaborate game that she loved to play involved showing them all the things that shamed them, terrified them, and broke their hearts. Then she would sup from that cloud of dark energy until she was as bloated as a greedy tick.

The Blood Maiden built up a small fire in the gravel floor, and as she laid over it a bushel of dried foliage, they ignited, causing them to smolder. Smoke soon filled the tiny house. The sorceress kept the flames small as not to frighten the Nagual. Alissa felt as if she might suffocate as her lungs were invaded by the thick plumes stinking like burning plastic. The miniature corpse marionettes were split open and their entrails spilled out to the waiting Nagual before their remains were cast upon the flames, with their flesh ravaged from their bones. Soon nothing but ash and a caustic stench were left of their existence. The Nagual ran a claw-tipped finger through the small bloody piles as it began to seek the spirits nearby. Alissa watched as its features began to change, transforming into a very familiar countenance.

"I'm so scared," Kelly cried.

Alissa wept, unable to speak.

"I want to go home."

The Nagual's skin had morphed into a scaly mockery of Kelly's face.

"I'm so sorry." Alissa sobbed through the smoke to the shapeshifter channeling her lost friend.

"Why did we come on this stupid trip? I should be at home," Kelly said. "It's your fault, you know. It's all your fault   that   I'm   dead!"

CHAPTER FIFTEEN

Wes shambled forward, half of his right foot went over a slippery edge, and his weight followed it as he fell. He threw his arms out as his body twisted in a desperate attempt to right the wrong he had just committed in his exhaustion. It was the same mistake that nearly took Alissa's life. He managed to grasp the slick stone ledge a moment before plunging into the pit completely. It slowed his momentum enough to spare his life as his bare feet became impaled upon the tips of sharp spikes. His chest and abdomen slammed against the pit wall only to stick there upon a mass of climbing vines covered in spines. His agonizing cries delighted his onlookers as he pulled his feet free. Wes held his breath in an attempt to rein himself in, as he needed to focus on something other than the pain. His minded drifted beyond the black room to memories of living in the world above. He knew his arms wouldn't have the

strength left to pull himself back up onto the floor if he
didn't act quickly, yet the only way of gaining enough
traction to push with his feet while pulling with his hands
would be stabbing his already mangled soles on the thorny
pit wall. Wes had no other choice, as he felt his arms
turning to gelatin. He lifted his feet, paused to ready
himself, then screamed until his throat felt as if it was
being torn free with each step up the rungs of torment. He
dragged himself back onto the temple floor shaking and his
feet felt raw as he brought his hand down to remove a thorn
lodged in his flesh. The Blood King issued a throaty shriek
bringing Wes up onto his hands and knees to desperately
feel out a pathway around the pit before him.

He crawled along as quickly as he could while still
being cautious and he found the pit took up the entire
center of the black room. Wes creeped along the wall and
discovered a four-inch-wide ledge edging the hole. It would
force him to stand up then to walk upon his tip toes with his
back against the wall. His heart sank to the bottom of his
gut, burying his resolve in sickening defeat. Blood Bringer
refused to let the game end so quickly. He crept up in the
blackness to grip Wes by the throat. He brought the young
man within inches of his mouth then roared before

slamming Wes against the wall. Wes shot back onto his feet, and screaming, he began to cross the pit, each stride shakily agonizing. He worried his footing would give way or he might slip upon his own blood. Wes knew what awaited him within the pit, and his feet reminded him every step of the way.

****

Shadow Priestess peeked through the window but all she could see was smoke. She could hear Alissa weeping somewhere within the plumes of gray but she had yet to spot her. The shifted face of the Nagual came into view as the voice of a dead girl drifted from her lipless mouth.

"Who's that shadow you're following? She could be trying to kill you, like how I got killed. Maybe she'll cut your skin off..."

Alissa didn't answer, her lungs were seizing up, burning with a lack of oxygen. Kelly's words did eat at her. Was it possible the shadow woman had led her there just for that purpose? Alissa coughed, then wheezed as she fought for breath. Blood Maiden was busy fanning the flaming pile of dried foliage and loosening her jaws like a snake preparing to swallow a mouse when a shadow crept through the window.

"You're already dead, Alissa. As soon as you stepped foot here you were dead," Kelly said.

"Wes just didn't want to scare you, but you're dead already. Can't you feel yourself dying?"

The Blood Maiden could taste the smoke was laden with fear and remorse; the girl's blood was almost ready to be shed and fed upon.

Alissa wrenched her wrists and could feel the thorns as they were being pulled through her skin. She yelped as she struggled to free herself. A familiar voice spoke into her ear; the words she did not know yet the sentiment was felt. She gritted her teeth as she was freed of the restraints keeping her bound to the stake. Alissa darted through the smoke, then kicked the embers of the fire upon the Nagual and Blood Maiden. She screamed as she flung them with her foot up into the sorceress's face then bolted for the door, but before she could pull it free a smoldering Nagual leaped upon her back, sinking its teeth into her shoulder. Alissa threw her head back, bashing the creature in the mouth. It released her and she got to her feet. She stumbled forward, screaming, as she found the door. Alissa grabbed Wes's pack as she ran into the cool darkness beyond the door, choking lungsful of air into her body.

Shadow Priestess could be seen against the gray smoke. Blood Maiden leaped at her, opening her mouth so wide that it became a black void, hungry for energy, shrieking in a rage. The Nagual rushed after the human who could be heard hacking up mouthfuls of black mucous outside the sorceress's dwelling. The priestess darted away from the soot-covered necromancer as the burning cinders Alissa had sent into the thatched wooden roof of the sorceress's hovel ignited, burning ferociously above them.

The reptilian shapeshifter pursued Alissa as she ran, rounding the house as the roof began to burn. Before her was the rippling of dark water and the roaring of a waterfall beckoned to her. The creature hesitated, hissing as the flames grew higher, and spread to the tree leaning over Blood Maiden's house. Alissa remembered how her lantern kept it at bay so she stopped on the bank of the water, then picked up a heavy black stone before running back towards the flaming house. The Nagual came to meet her in battle, jumping at her chest, but Alissa brought the rock up to bash it in its scaly face as she gripped its shoulder. It fell, momentarily subdued, as Alissa retrieved a burning piece of wood that tumbled from the fiery roof. She turned triumphantly, waving the fire into the creature's face, driving it back until it retreated to the dark, cold forest.

Shadow Priestess emerged from the fire, rushing to Alissa. She whistled to the girl, hoping she would follow quickly. Blood Maiden was blinded, her eyelids scorched shut, yet she found her way out of the inferno. She screeched in a rage into the smoke filling the air. Shadow Priestess knew the powerful sorceress wouldn't be useless for long and the retribution sought would be something neither could escape.

****

The Wayobs were soaked with blood from the crimson river. The two of them returned to hunt for the girl's soggy corpse. They dove into the currents in the area that she was last spotted in, succumbing to the rushing flow. The one dressed in Kelly's skin emerged, slapping the surface in frustration as he sloshed his way to the river bed. He had seen her go under with his own eyes, and the only way that she could have made it out would have been by the aid of the mischief maker, the shadow priestess and her tribe of skeleton coats. His partner hopped out onto the bank to shake his feathers dry while the leader cursed in their foul tongue. The scent of fire filled their nostrils and in the distance a plume of smoke rose above the withering trees. Blood Bringer's daughter never let her flames grow that large, as it would frighten her creature away. They looked to one another and nodded, then took to the air. The journey would not be long until they would discover the source of the fire. They readied themselves to bring a valuable trophy back to their master, another human to be tested or cut open atop the pyramid...and maybe coax Shadow Priestess back as well.

****

Alissa struggled to keep moving as she dove into the freezing waters pooling beneath the waterfall. It stole her breath, yet it felt refreshing, and it jolted her awake as they made their way into its black depths. She swam, though she could not see her guardian, and the shadow woman kept whistling softly until they emerged on the farther shore.

Alissa was freezing, her clothing drenched, yet her adrenaline was pumping through her body at maximum capacity. Alissa climbed up onto a boulder to retrieve an undying torch, it was clear to her then she would be venturing back into the hidden caverns of the earth, but after all she had just been through, she found the arms of the mountain welcoming.

****

Wes inched his way along sideways, his calf muscles were in absolute torment. The balls of his feet bled freely, the flesh burned in the open holes going clean through his feet like the wounds of the stigmata. He hardly risked breathing at all as he moved slowly, an inch at a time, for fear the ledge might disappear from under him, leaving him to be impaled upon the spikes below. When at last his toe felt the forgiveness of the stone floor wide enough to accommodate an entire foot he wept out loud. Once Wes stood both feet on solid ground, he used a foot to feel about him to be certain he was in a safe place before lying on the opposite side of the pit, his body wracked with terrible shaking. A macabre cheering echoed across to him. They were watching his painful progress like some sort of sporting event, delighting in his struggle. He crawled forward across the black floor to where a glowing seal could be discerned and a doorway. Wes put his hand against it, it was frigid. The stone slid away from beneath his palm, opening to another room.

Wes stood to peer inside. Though he had seen spirits who walked in the flesh, unbelievable monsters, and pyramids within mountains, he could not believe he was gazing into a room filled with snow, and freezing gales threw sleet into his eyes. Wes looked down at his nearly naked body, realizing it would not take long to freeze to death in a place so unforgiving, a place where it was so cold it burned his skin. A hand shoved him inside, and he turned to retreat, yet sorcery prevented him from passing the threshold. Ah-Puch scoffed from the other side of the doorway, taunting him by sticking his decaying hand through the door, then drawing it back again. The holes in Wes's feet ached almost instantly, making it much more difficult to walk. He trudged into the white powder, realizing it grew deeper the farther he walked. He decided to try to make it to the wall on his left hand side, then skirt it to the other side of the room. The snow was waist-deep, prompting Wes to have to crawl over the top of it. His arms sunk deep into it, stinging his flesh. The winds picked up again, throwing freezing slush in his face as once more he clawed onward. His teeth chattered together violently as he fought his way to the wall. The snow kept falling heavily; he had only rested momentarily when he found himself nearly buried alive where he sat. Wes made his way forward along the wall, falling deeper and deeper into the smothering sheets of white. He hadn't even breached the midway point when his extremities had already gone completely numb. Fear gripped him as he pushed himself to keep going. He knew if he grew too tired he would be swallowed up in the mouth of winter fixed to close around him. The harder he struggled, the more he found himself falling into the growing drifts of blinding white. The torches cast flickering blue shadows through the storm raging within the room. He pulled a torch from the wall, passed his palm over its fire. The pale flame crackled as it warmed his hand, he could feel the numbness subsiding. Hope sparked within his heart.

****

It was nearly impossible for Alissa to see the shadow woman within the black chambers of the earth. Only when she passed through the blue torchlight did she stand out against the obsidian walls. She did whistle occasionally to remind the girl she did not journey alone. Soon she would part ways from Alissa in order to breach the pyramid temple in an effort to gather the young man who had been captured. The priestess meant to speak with her shadow-coated spy in the hopes Wes had been spotted alive. She knew with every moment that passed the likelihood of saving his life was dwindling, yet the priestess would not give up. Her mischief had been felt before with the sealing of the portal to her people. The parade of flesh had slowed tremendously in Xibalba since her ritual suicide, but occasionally to the lord's delight, some poor soul found their way in through caves of other lands. Shadow Priestess, along with her simian companions, took great joy in ruining his celebrations. She was an outlaw in the lands of fear. One Ah-Puch would pay a hefty reward to capture.

The cave systems all intertwined with one another. The cold, dark river emptied out behind Blood Maiden's hovel and flowed through most of them as well. Alissa was still chilled and damp, yet the pace the shadow woman kept made her muscles burn with exertion. Alissa felt an urgency radiating from the entity and it put her on edge with the thoughts of the massive centipede she had encountered when she was still with Wes. The passageway in which she traveled with the shadow woman echoed with the roaring river that wasn't far from them, rambling through an adjacent cavern. She fought to keep moving. Her mind was haunted with the faces of her companions, their voices in her head devastated her, bringing tears to her eyes. Alissa kept moving. It was all she could do.

Shadow Priestess watched the girl weeping as she soldiered onward. It reminded her of a time centuries ago when she struggled to keep her small tribe together and thriving. The hopelessness she had felt of trying to keep them from the hands of death and in watching as women mourned the loss of their husbands and sons daily. It would all happen again to those walking in the lands of the living, as control of the gateway had been forfeited to Ah-Puch. It troubled the priestess greatly to think that the demon lords could come and go freely to hunt the world above once more.

The passageway opened into a grand cavern, where many corridors converged. It would be their point of separation though Alissa was not aware of it yet. Water pooled in its center reflecting the beauty of a tapestry of phosphorescent moss clinging to the walls. Alissa gripped the torch as the priestess showed her the way over slick rocks to an opening just big enough for her to squeeze through. She hesitated there, gazing down into the glimmering pool beside her; startled by her reflection. Alissa brought a hand up to her face to tug at her pale cheeks. Her lips were violet, she could see it clearly even in the poor light and she looked like a corpse.

CHAPTER SIXTEEN

Wes brought the torch down into the snow before him, its flame snuffed out slowly. It was a meager attempt at burning out a pathway, but he soon realized he was making miniscule headway, yet it was progress nonetheless. His body cried for warmth for even though his arms and legs were numb, his torso burned painfully. The warmth frightened him; hypothermia was said to make people feel hot, prompting victims to shed their clothing. He hoped then the maggot that had feverishly sought to make his body its home was now freezing to death. Wes reminded himself he was already almost naked but for the crusted layer of Mayan Blue slathered over him. He began to feel confused, clumsy, almost as if he were drunk, yet another sign of freezing to death. He used the dead torch like a shovel to toss snow aside. It spared his hands a bit, and slowly he gained ground. Wes made it at last to the far side of the winter room to find no doorway in the wall, the exit still hidden to him. His legs were so frozen they no longer heeded the directions his frantic brain sent them, and he fell onto his stomach. Wes's face burned, he could feel his skin splitting on his cheeks. The torch lay upon the bed of frost beneath him. His eyes caught a faint glow, from beneath the slush. Frantically he dug down, scooping up armloads of wet snow revealing a bright radiance. He had shoveled enough to have dug his own grave if he failed. There in front of him was a small square cut out of the stone, beyond it shown with blue light. The exit hole was lined with sharp spines, waiting to strip the skin from his body. Wes didn't contemplate it, he pulled himself through the booby-trapped exit and felt his flesh being peeled away in numb ribbons. He was bathed in warmth on the other side, both from the lack of snow and his own blood running from his wounds. He stood up on trembling legs. The room was filled with broken bodies; some wore tattered clothing of different civilizations. It reminded Wes of how many had failed within the temple and how many centuries men were forced to their deaths by the Lord of Xibalba. The large basin in the center of the room burned brightly with a blue blaze. He came upon a corpse wearing a dusty chest plate and he guessed it to be a conquistador's armor. Wes brushed the buildup of time away while he wondered how the warrior had made it so far in such heavy gear. The face reflected back at him was nothing more than a sickening confirmation to a question he had asked himself when the maggot so ravenously sought to climb into his wound. His face was crusted tight with Mayan Blue paint, yet his jowls hung with the absence of true existence, and his eyes were clouded over with death. Wes was trapped somewhere between life and true death in a state of unending torment. He recalled Alissa asking if they had found their way into Hell, and in that moment he believed they actually had.

****

A shadowy hand covered her eyes, trying to focus Alissa's attention on thoughts other than her own reflection. Alissa's head swam with the voices of Wes and Kelly and both had proclaimed her dead already. The priestess projected an image of herself before she made her self-sacrifice, beautiful and serene. She hummed a soothing tune then raised her hand and placed it over her heart. Slowly Alissa did the same, resting her shaking hand over her own chest. Alissa could feel her own heartbeat, it calmed her a bit.

"Not dead...not yet," Alissa wept.

She followed as the silhouette slipped through the thin crack into a smaller chamber. It had one larger opening on its opposite side. The priestess motioned to her to squat upon the cave floor. They were waiting for something, yet Alissa did not know what. She sat the torch down on its side next to her then opened the pack that she had been carrying, hoping to find a granola bar or anything to eat. Alissa stuck her hand all the way to the bottom of the bag, where her fingers passed over a circular object. She pulled it out and unwrapped the disc. The priestess spoke excitedly in her own tongue; the disc could seal the door again, but yet her own blood had already been drained. The blood of the young woman could be used, but she hoped that Alissa would be spared an eternity in Xibalba unlike her when she had chosen in desperation. She placed her hand over the young woman's eyes and shared with her the last moments of her people and her final sacrifice. The vision wrenched Alissa's heart at the sight of the two young boys, their throats opening, spilling their innocent blood. It then morphed to show Alissa the chamber in which they sat before spanning out into the cave systems, following a path through the darkness and ending in a drop into what looked like a pit or pool. At the very bottom was a long tunnel, like a throat, and it was lined with bones. She could feel the priestess's thoughts.

"Is that the way out?" Alissa asked as it burned into her memory.

Her voice ricocheted off the stone walls as she deposited the artifact back into the backpack. The shadow motioned for Alissa, and though she could see no expression, she knew the entity wished for her to continue alone on the path shown to her in the vision. Alissa could feel it as clear as a spoken direction. She knew the spirit would not be swayed, the Shadow Priestess radiated a determined aura after seeing the disc, as perhaps she knew that time was running out. She only prayed the shadow woman meant to find Wes, to guide him as she had Alissa. Her companion slipped into the darkness of the exit before she could beg her to stay. She was alone to recall the map that had committed itself to her memory. Her path appeared to follow a westerly route, passing many smaller off-shooting caverns, climbing up then gradually leading back down to a flat area and then a deep drop. Alissa gripped the torch, walked to the threshold of the exit, then took a deep breath before letting its indigo light lead her into the void beyond the tiny chamber.

****

The Wayob hunters landed upon the shore of the waterfall beside the decimated home of the Blood Maiden. They found the sorceress nursing a sightless face. She sensed them immediately, then told them of a human girl and the shadow woman who guided her through the forest. She heard the young woman splash into the dark water behind her hovel. The owl men knew that she had escaped into the caves behind the waterfall. They left the witch cursing the two that had destroyed her dwelling, shaking her fists, beseeching the Wayob to avenge her as they crept into the mouth of the cave.

****

Wes was startled by a rush of whispering voices, some of them weeping wildly. They spun around him ferociously in a cacophony of despair. He could discern one specifically for it spoke in Spanish, a language he had learned in school. It was of a young man, begging for death. A raucous laughter tailed the echoes of the dead, the Lord of

Death and his lieges taking great pleasure in the suffering of every soul that found itself trapped in their realm. The corpses lay long rotten and still, as they must have gotten what they asked for. The room still held the grief of their last moments, the mocking amusement their tears elicited from the King of Xibalba. Hate burned in Wes's gut. He knew an entity such as Ah-Puch could not be slain, yet Wes resigned himself to the fact he would never bow to him or beg for death.

A throaty growl issued from the other side of the fire, and an eye shine caught Wes's attention. A feline head came into view, massive in size, snarling hungrily at the human as it entered its lair. Wes stood absolutely still as the jaguar dashed the stone floor before it with its claws. He knew it was going to come for him, and that the size of its teeth would certainly rend the flesh from his bones with little effort. He worried then he would be eaten alive, feeling himself being devoured mouthful by gory mouthful without the mercy of death, and it made his extremities feel as if he were buried in snow once more. The giant cat leaped the basin of fire, landing lightly upon its paws. It began pacing before him, snarling, its stout body decorated with dark spots upon its slick tawny coat. Wes inched backwards causing the cat to follow him, and he attempted to put a pile of dead bodies between him and the cat, but it moved too quickly. The jaguar jumped onto his chest, forcing him onto his back. The sheer bulk of it was crushing, as it easily outweighed Wes, who was not a large-framed man. He threw his arm up defensively as the cat went for his face. His wrist became locked in its powerful jaws, and the sounds of his bones being snapped in his face sent his other hand around to punch the cat in the side of its skull. His beating had no effect on the beast as it shook its head, shredding his flesh within its mouth. Claws dug into his chest causing Wes to panic. His own weeping in his ears reminded him of the others who failed to exit the stone room. He reached over to grab an arm bone of a fallen warrior and he wielded it like a club to bash the cat over the snout. It released him, bounding back to stalk him as he bled upon the floor. It readied itself for another attack and so did Wes. Its claws met his hips as it lunged in to bite his abdomen, and Wes stuck the bone into its mouth. The jaguar snapped it in two before being pushed off balance by the human beneath it, but it rebounded instantly to leap once again for his face. Wes brought the jagged bone up like a primitive dagger into the cat's throat. The cat tore strips of flesh from Wes's chest with its claws as it tumbled away yowling in torment. It retreated to the darkness in a far corner of the chamber. Wes could smell its blood; he could smell his own too mixed with the scent of primal fear. The animal was in the midst of dying when a doorway opened upon the far wall. Ah-Puch entered, in his train followed two of his lieges, demonic kings Wes knew were taking great delight in watching him be tortured. The Lord of Xibalba looked to his prized cat, then to the human who had put it down. In the king's eyes, Wes could see ire rising, knowing he dealt a blow to his tormentor. It strengthened him for the hell awaiting him.

****

She was very petite, yet she had the true presence of a warrior. Skeleton Queen, the leader of the skeleton coats, had spied upon the hunters as they toted the human along, strung up like a wild boar to a tree limb. Shadow Priestess would be expecting her in the voids so she hustled through the tree tops with a guard of two males in her trail. They traversed the dead jungle very quickly, making their way to the honeycombed cavern wall with all haste. They nimbly scampered up to one of the highest cave entrances to take their places and await the arrival of the priestess. From their view, they could see the pyramid temple, atop it clustered a group of Wayobs, all squawking greedily as they fought each other for unidentifiable pieces of carrion. The abandoned ball court sat empty to one side of the pyramid, as rarely was a game played there for most captives were slaughtered hastily. Behind the temple was the pathway to the cavern housing the cenote, a deep sacrificial well that held the skeletal remains of many. Its waters were a dark cobalt hue from the ample amounts of Mayan Blue deposited there from the skin of those who were fed to the blue maw. The sentries took their posts at the cave entrance while the queen descended into the heart of the mountain alone to converse in a secret chamber with the shadow woman.

****

Alissa was alone, only the sound of her breathing echoed back from the passageway walls and could be heard, for the river tributary was but a trickle in the cavern she walked. Her hand gripping the blue-flamed torch felt numb, and she realized she was growing increasingly cold. When Alissa left the world above, chasing after the lost professor beside Wes, she hadn't thought to equip herself with anything more than what she wore to sleep which were her jeans and t-shirt. She thought of her supplies in the land of the living, the cell phones that were zipped up in a bag that had been tattered by mutant bird men. She shivered thinking of the owl-headed creatures now having free reign in the Georgia forests; how many more people would fall victim to them?

Alissa continued in the path the vision left in her mind; avoiding the off-shooting passageways. After what felt like hours, she stopped to rest. Alissa had no idea what time it was in the above world, only that she had managed maybe a few hours of sleep on the bank of the blood river. She hadn't eaten since the time she spent beside the campfire watching Wes study the disc that was painted Mayan Blue. Her stomach growled, then rolled, with hunger pains, another sign she wasn't completely dead yet. There was nothing around her but black stone, not a single edible item to be found. It had been a long while since she had even seen a hint of glowing moss though it would take much more than painful protesting on her stomach's part to even attempt to eat that. Alissa drew a few deep breaths. The air was cold in her lungs and strangely it calmed her. The cavern she now journeyed through was different than the one in which she and Wes had been trapped, and it felt much easier to breathe. Even as the walls closed in about her, Alissa had yet to feel the crushing claustrophobia of the other passages. She hoped it was a sign she was being brought closer to the surface, and perhaps a way back into the sunshine and forest winds. That thought got her back onto her feet to keep fighting onward.

****

Wes refused to flinch or show any fear to the Lord of Xibalba. The lord advanced upon the human whose hands were drenched in jaguar blood, knowing this one would not choose death as the roomful of other corpses had done. Beyond his irritation he knew this human was a spirit of great fortitude, one fitting enough to send into the blue mouth.

Wes watched as a short, fat liege waddled forward, his skin covered in festering lesions, and tugged at Ah-Puch's elbow. He stood up on his tiptoes to whisper a secret to his king who nodded approvingly. The Lord of Death pointed a boney finger to Wes, then motioned him through the doorway along with what sounded like a haughty laugh. The stubby plague king came shuffling over, holding his hand out as if to help guide the young man. The stink of him as he came closer turned Wes's gut and he refused to touch the outstretched palm of the festering king, instead walking a wide circle around him on his way to the open passageway.

The room beyond howled with raging winds. Wes was on guard after the king's reaction to the pus king's surreptitious words; he waited for the worst. Wes was pushed inside, and instantly the gales nearly knocked him to the ground. The force of them drove his breath back into his lungs as he laughed defiantly.

"Is this all you got?"

CHAPTER SEVENTEEN

A pain in his shoulder blade sent him to his knees, and his blood ran in a hot trail down his back. Amongst the din of the winds he looked to see a dagger lodged there in his back. It had penetrated deeply, up to its hilt, before halting. His breathing became labored as he struggled to stand against the wind. Wes had just regained his stance when something dashed by his head. There was a second of burning pain, then a rush of warmth down the side of his head. Wes lifted his fingers to discover his ear was missing. Rage built inside of him and drowned out the pain. Their degradation would truly last until his absolute end...if it ever truly came.

****

Shadow Priestess drew near to the hidden chamber where she would convene with the Skeleton Queen, as she needed to know the state of the human, though she didn't doubt that once inside the temple his condition grew much more dismal. The young man would have to learn the lesson eventually to ignore his suffering or his torment would leave him completely insane, a putrid thing groveling at the foot of the temple for scraps of flesh, envious of all who still held a shred of humanity. Xibalba was a land of living ghosts, hungry to absorb anything resembling life, whether flesh, blood, or energy, leaving the priestess along with her tribe of skeleton coats to be the only bearers of mercy in the realm of fear.

Shadow Priestess whistled up the black passageway to hear a soft squeak in reply, and her consort awaited her patiently. She walked without a torch, and the tunnels could be traced solely by memory now after centuries of exploring them. Above the doorway to the dark chamber grew a patch of green moss, casting a soft green glow into its entrance.

The priestess stepped inside unconcerned, when soft paws padded across the stone floor. The simian queen perched upon a ledge beside her to greet her with soft peeping. They usually exchanged pleasantries this way before the passing of information. She positioned her other hand over the tiny primate's head before casting her mind into the thoughts of Skeleton Queen. It was the only shamanistic power she retained from her human life, one she was grateful the gods did not strip from her when her flesh was cast aside. The priestess could see the hunting party carrying their trophy to the pyramid and watched him choking upon the meager contents of his stomach. A sense of emergency crept over her shadowed form; he would have to be a strong spirit to withstand the trials. Shadow Priestess released her confidant to return to her tribe amongst the dead jungle, knowing if the young man did not give in he would most certainly be cast into the blue maw and that was an event she hoped to intervene in. It seemed the end would be coming for the young woman and her companion soon, and she just prayed release would be granted to them both.

****

The blades like flying razors came at him from different angles all invisible to his eyes until they met his flesh. They varied in size, leaving weeping holes dispersed about his body. Wes pulled them free with tormented cries each time only to keep moving forward through the raging winds. He realized he was only in the midst of a death march now, that he would not die unless he begged for it, but that was an act he refused to fulfill. At the midpoint of the long rectangular room the tumult died instantly, leaving him wary and shaking in faint torch light. His body was a mess of blue paint lined with blood, tracing its way down to his mangled feet. Above him in the darkness, his good ear perceived a barely audible clicking sound and what followed was a cloud of moving blackness, screeching, and hungrily seeking his blood. He was engulfed in flapping leathery wings and fangs. The attackers went directly for his open dagger lacerations, their greedy mouths feasting upon Wes. As he tore each one of them away, they were only replaced by another ravenous maw. The bats seemed motivated with an unnatural thirst, a product of being creatures of Xibalba. He soon became overcome by them as they sunk their teeth into every inch of his skin. Wes fell to the stone floor, kicking at the voracious storm sweeping around him. His head was filled with the din of their screeching as they opened fresh gashes to feed from. He rolled wildly across the ground feeling a few of the bats being crushed to dust beneath him. Wes ripped one from his arm, and in the torch light he stared into its decrepit face, and saw its eyes were hollow holes. He understood then they were not living bats at all, but more akin to those decrepit beings crowded around the pyramid when the hunters hauled him in, undead creatures with an insatiable hunger. He also reminded himself he too was becoming one, and it filled him with rabid fury. He pushed himself to his feet before violently throwing himself against the walls, hurling his back against pillars, and tearing off bat heads with his own mouth.

****

Alissa stumbled along, passing dark, empty chambers she dared not enter with only a torch as protection. Though she could breathe easily she couldn't help but feel she was being watched through nocturnal eyes. The encompassing black was an entity all itself just waiting to slowly swallow her whole. Alissa's shadow appeared distorted upon the walls of the caverns in the torch light, her vision was blurring in the constant half-light. She grew so weary of constantly being afraid, she was frightened of the dark tunnels, of the lands beyond the caves, of anything dwelling within the haunted realm of Xibalba. It was sickeningly exhausting. A low drumming caught her ear, so faint upon first hearing, she thought it was only a phantom of her imagination. Alissa continued down the cold passageway only to find the rhythmic thrumming grew louder until soon it clamored like an enormous heartbeat. It slowed her pace, for each time it sounded she could feel her chest aching as if a knife had been thrust through her breastbone. She cried out in agony. A figure stood over her, looking down as she writhed, and it wore the tattered face of Kelly.

****

The Wayob stalked silently down the black passageways. The scent of the young woman drew them along, she was close, they knew it. The sacred drumming began, they halted to listen closely. A scream echoed down the tunnels, they hurried to it in greedy excitement, knowing their reward would be grand.

****

The Lord of Xibalba entered the chamber of razors, followed by his gruesome entourage. Wes grinned as he stomped the final living dead bat into dust beneath his barefoot. As Ah-Puch motioned to Blood Bringer and Bone King, they stepped forward. Wes readied himself, unwilling to be taken easily again. He needlessly raised his fists in defense as a thump echoed through the stone room. The drum boomed once more, bringing Wes to his knees. With each pound it felt as if his heart would stop beating or explode from his chest. From the shadows stepped the skeleton-faced shaman, a leather strap affixed around his shoulder allowing him to carrying a great drum with human skin stretched over its head. His hand beat the drum slowly, and its call resembled the pulse in Wes's temples. Wes put his hands over his ears yet he could still feel its percussion in his chest, as it pounded in time with his heart. The demon lieges came to collect him with satisfied grins. As the shaman slowed his pace Wes's chest ached. His arteries struggled for a moment before his heart seized like a clenched fist. The drumming was so powerful it reverberated off all of the stone walls within the lands of Xibalba, signaling to all dwelling there the blue maw would soon be fed.

****

At the thump of the drums the priestess knew she was far too late to extricate the young man from the death lord's temple. He had survived the trials. His reward would be being fed to the blue mouth, which was a true honor in the eyes of the ghoulish inhabitants of the land of fear for it signified the fortitude of his spirit. She was crushed by the feeling of loss, now that the drumming started there was no way for Alissa and Wes to leave Xibalba, they would decay the instant they set foot in the living world again. Shadow Priestess screamed in defeat. She turned back to search for the girl, straining over great boulders holding up tons of earth and stone above her, then through crevasses. Twice she cried out yet she knew the girl would not understand her so she reverted to whistling in a vain attempt to catch Alissa's attention. In the distance a crying alerted her to the presence she sought. The girl was fading so quickly she too would become nothing but a walking corpse very soon, seeking to instill fear and torment in the living. Each time the drum echoed up the tunnel she knew it was killing the girl, along with Wes, stopping their hearts slowly.

****

They found her lying on her side, her fingers jammed into her ears. The Wayobs hustled to claim her as the drumming shook the caverns of Xibalba. They were filled with excitement knowing that Ah-Puch was about to feed the blue maw. The ritual was always announced by the heart drum and culminated at the edge of the grand cenote in the caverns behind the pyramid temple. The master would remove the young man's heart after the final tolling of the drum, then push him into the pool below, and when he re-emerged he would be nothing more than a hungry corpse with skin of bright blue. They hadn't witnessed such a ceremony in ages, and they hurried to be among the crowd. The Wayobs pounced on Alissa as she struggled through agonizing pain. They gripped her arms before dragging her through the tunnels, making their way towards one of the cavern openings. She fought feebly, slapping at the creatures as they pulled her along. Alissa cried out as the drumbeat assaulted her once more, leaving her too weak to break free.

CHAPTER EIGHTEEN

Wes was forced along amongst the group of demon kings as Ah-Puch led the procession down the steep steps of the pyramid. The drumming continued to stab into him, clenching his heart like a tightening vice. He could sense the end was near, a sickening release from the torment he had endured. The crowd gathering at the bottom of the stairs shrieked eagerly as he was paraded by. A beating of wings above him told him the Wayobs had joined the train. He hobbled along upon aching feet, skin itching with Mayan Blue pigment. The broken stone structures around him were lit with faint torch light, a city of desolation decaying just as slowly as its inhabitants. A chunk of broken roadway was picked up then tossed at his face by a mummified onlooker. His blood brought them great satisfaction for they howled in triumph as it burned his eyes. This prompted a handful of other malevolent creatures to do the same, stoning him with any debris their decrepit hands could attain. A flitting shadow caught his stinging eye, and it leaped from a rooftop of a ruined tomb before disappearing completely. He prayed the skeleton-coated monkeys had come to free him yet he knew such small beings could only do so much. The path his executioners followed took them around the perimeter of the great pyramid, into a crop of rocky rises leading up to the pitted cavern wall. They climbed an uneven trail up the stony steps, then into a cavern opening that looked like the fanged mouth of a predator. The passages echoed with the drum, its thrumming painfully resonated within Wes's chest. He fell to his knees only to be kicked in the back, then dragged back onto his feet. The tunnel behind him erupted with shouting as the walking dead spectators screeched with impatience. It felt as if they had walked for miles in the black caves before they came to an opening. Wes stumbled as he was pushed up a set of steps, and in utter darkness the demon kings ascended to the platform before the cenote's edge. Their journey was punctuated by the beating of the great drum, and it slowed to nearly nothing as they prepared their ritual. A conch shell trumpeted across the surface of the water below, a perfectly circular pool became visible as a thousand blue-flamed torches leaped to life at the command of Ah-Puch. Wes gazed down upon it as it looked like a great cold moon cast in a black sky and he began to tremble uncontrollably. A crowd began to gather about the brim of the blue maw. Some climbed onto separate cliffs across from the procession, shrieking excitedly. Professor Lipton was among them. Wes felt sickening anger when his eyes fell upon the traitorous corpse of the old man and thought if only he had not broken the seal. The pain in Wes's chest was nearly crippling, and only his stubborn rage kept him from begging for death.

****

The drumming was the signal; she had witnessed it before. It was the instrument bringing about the change from living to living dead. The priestess was immune to it due to her self-sacrifice just as the other dead residents of Xibalba, but most of her skeleton-coated companions hid from it in fear, knowing their tiny hearts might not withstand it. The girl would not last long. Shadow Priestess rushed up the tunnel, realizing there were two winged figures standing over Alissa. They grabbed her arms and roughly dragged her down the passageway. She was too late. Alissa's weak cries echoing from the stone walls surrounded the priestess, filling her with defeat. The priestess knew Alissa and Wes would be united soon, she only hoped she could find release for them both. She knew the fastest way through the tunnels would be the river raging through them. She had no fear of drowning because she was already dead. Shadow Priestess no longer had to travel cautiously like she did while protecting the human so she made her way to the black rapids and cast herself into them.

****

The Skeleton Queen perched in the top of a withered tree. The first beat of the drum sent her tribe running for cover. The instrument was attuned to the human hearts beating within the lands of fear yet her fragile simian heart felt it as well. In the past a few of her elders had succumbed to it as the sacrifices were drawn towards death. The creatures of Xibalba moved towards the great pounding, knowing the blue maw would soon be satiated. A shriek of victory caught her attention as her eyes focused in the distance. Two of the owl men carried the young woman, and each had her by the wrists wrapped in their talons, hooting with excitement. They flew quickly with powerful beats of their wings over the forests and rivers, heading for a cavern opening leading to the cenote and its gruesome festivities. She leaped down to swing through the limbs of the tree until she landed on the black soil, like a burial ground it always felt freshly turned. Xibalba was nothing more than an open grave. Skeleton Queen called to her guards who came in an instant. She could see the fear in their eyes when she signaled to them to make ready for war.

****

Alissa hung from the clawed feet of the Wayob as they flew her out of the cavern. She could see the dead forest below, the diseased river soon passed quickly beneath her. They veered over the blood river, adjusting their course to fly in the direction of the excruciating drumming. Alissa's heart thundered in her chest, matching its rhythm. The ruins of the city and the bloody pyramid came into view; beyond them from a gaping hole in the cavern wall thundered the ritualistic pulse. Alissa knew their destination was in the cave that resembled the fanged mouth of a hungry beast. A line of blue-skinned dead was already making their way into it. The Wayobs called down to the throng, and the creatures shrieked at the sight of the sacrifice they carried. The crowds made way for the triumphant hunters as they landed to present the girl to their master. She was carried down a dark tunnel, as the drum endlessly pounded in her chest.

****

The torturous rhythm felt unending; the shaman beat his drum at the young man's back for what felt like an eternity as the master of Xibalba waited for his people to gather for the ceremony. Wes heard the excitement raised by the Wayobs as they fluttered over his head into the expansive cavern. The Lord of Death and his demon kings shouted, pointing their bony fingers in the direction of the Wayob and the prize they presented. The crowds of the underworld cheered eagerly. His eyes filled with tears when he saw Alissa and that she hung limp from their feet. If it weren't for her terrified face he would have thought she was already dead. The owl men hovered above the cenote before flying the girl back to lay her at the feet of Ah-Puch. The shaman behind him continued to kill the pace of the drum, and his heart died slowly with it. He looked to the tattered blue corpses, faces grinning with rictor, who waited for him to become like them. Those that hadn't deteriorated beyond recognition all bore the same hole in their chests, hearts removed in ritual sacrifice and their skin blue... like his. Wes lifted a shaking hand, and it was anointed with a blue pigment. It once intrigued him; he now felt nauseated seeing it stain his flesh. The Lord of Death was given a dish, and he dipped his fingers in. The owl man who still wore Kelly's face over his own grabbed Alissa by her hair to present her face to Ah- Puch who anointed her with Mayan Blue, marking her as he had Wes. The Lord of Death drew his obsidian dagger, and then held it up to the hordes seated about the sinkhole. Wes refused to be cut open, to have his heart ripped from his chest or to watch it happen to Alissa. With the last ounce of his strength, Wes broke free of the demon kings and ran for the lip of the rocky step, dragging Alissa to her feet as he kicked the dead away. Wes leaped over the edge, taking Alissa with him. Their bodies hung for a second before gravity brought them into the waiting mouth of blue. The shouts of the Lord of Death became muffled as the water invaded his ear canals. Wes opened his eyes to see a form sinking before him. It was Alissa. He swam towards her, pulling himself deeper into the azure depths. His body felt weightless suspended in the cenote, his fear dissipated. The drumbeat became a vibration rippling through the water, and it swept over his skin before resonating in his chest. Wes knew soon it would end. He and Alissa would emerge from the pool as nothing more than hate-filled corpses if something wasn't done. A heavy splashing echoed into his ear, followed by another and then another. At first Wes thought the attendants were throwing heavy stones in hoping to pin him to the blue silt in the bottom of the cenote, yet he turned to see a skeletal face then understood they were coming for him.

The Lord of Xibalba demanded to cut the still hearts out of the human's chests, and his servants obeyed by diving into the maw.

CHAPTER NINETEEN

Alissa's air was knocked from her lungs upon impacting the surface of the blue pool. She sank quickly as her pack dragged her downward, and above her was a second figure. She recognized Wes, as he struggled to reach her but a barrage of other angry corpses came leaping into the blue water after them. Wes became entangled in them as she watched her breath bubbling up towards the surface from her opened mouth. She realized she was screaming.

The drumbeat pulsed through the water, slowing until Alissa thought it had stopped completely this time. She gripped her chest in a panic as the silhouette of Wes twisted in the water above her, and he fought the undead who came to return them to the cenote altar. Three of the creatures had him, tearing at his hair and bare flesh. Small shadows broke the surface of the pool, swimming quickly towards Wes as his body began to give out. Alissa watched the tiny warriors as they bit decrepit fingers off the hands of the living dead. They swarmed over the invaders, freeing Wes long enough for him to swim downward towards Alissa. She turned her head, and she could see the throat of the maw, the secret way out, but the hole swarmed with writhing skeletal arms, reaching out. They would never make it down the narrow passage without becoming entangled in them. Her hope died at the cloudy, blue bottom of the cenote.

****

Shadow Priestess became part of the water. It bore her a long way in a short amount of time. She exited the river when she spotted an opening in the cavern with pale torch light beyond it. The shrieking of the dead and the thrumming of the drum swept through her as she ran. She didn't even pause at the opening's edge, but she leapt out into the darkness before falling. She entered the pool alongside the winged figures of her enemies.

****

Wes grabbed Alissa by the arm just as she met the bottom of the blue maw. The silt erupted in an azure cloud as decrepit arms reached out from the cenote bed. The dead refused to cease their attack until Alissa and Wes were no longer human. Skeletal hands tangled in her hair, dragging her down as her lungs burned. She could feel the cold water waiting to invade her body. Wes tore at them, breaking them to pieces in desperation. He broke Alissa free, frantically looking for an escape from the hunters coming for them. There was a hole in the wall of the cenote, a tunnel of utter darkness. The water above them was filled with Wayobs and other living dead. A shadow darted to the tunnel entrance, but it was hardly discernable in the dark pool. It turned towards Wes, frantically beckoning for them to follow.

The Wayobs clawed at the surface of the blue maw, watching as the bodies of skeleton coat soldiers floated up lifeless. The skeleton coats were not strong swimmers. Their attack was a sacrifice to allow the humans an escape from the loyal dead who leaped into the cenote after them. The owl men splashed into the azure pool, then began powerfully pulling themselves downward towards the humans.

The shadow priestess darted deeper, powering ahead of the Wayob who clawed awkwardly through the water. She found the hidden exit of the cenote, only known to her through her centuries of exploration. The dead embedded in the pool clawed at the humans as she led them into the black passageway. The drum had slowed to the point that Wes hardly had the strength to pull Alissa along with him through the water. He felt his lungs burn in his aching chest. He could not see the silhouette before him, and cold water crept up his nostrils. Wes didn't think his body could handle the exertion as a thump of the drum ravaged him once more. His hand slipped from Alissa, he sought her frantically in the blackness around them. His lungs gave out, and a mouthful of cenote water invaded his throat. A faint whistling could be heard, muffled in his ears. Wes felt himself being yanked upward, his scalp impacted pure stone. Hands gripped the sides of his head as they fought to keep his mouth above the surface.

"Breathe," Alissa sputtered.

He realized they had been led to a small pocket of air in the water-filled tunnel. Alissa saved him by forcing him to the surface. There was barely a space big enough for their heads to be above the water. He inhaled, filling his lungs with breath. Wes coughed, then gulped more air into him.

'I'm almost blind down here. I can hardly see anything," he said.

The priestess passed her hand over Alissa's eyes, whispering softly.

"She'll guide us, listen for her whistling," Alissa said.

The drumming rippled through the cenote, battering their hearts. Alissa cried out, and Wes wrapped his arms around her. They clung to each other, waiting for the agony to subside long enough to keep swimming. The priestess disappeared once more. Wes and Alissa waited. Another whistle could be heard in the distance, and Alissa and Wes followed it.

They popped up to the shadow woman whistling like a bird. She sighed with relief when Alissa and Wes came up out of the water once more gasping for breath. They took a moment to fill their lungs, but when a gurgled screeching came from the tunnel behind them they knew the Wayobs had followed and found the air pocket. The shadow priestess left them. Wes and Alissa held their breath, hoping they would make it to the next pocket of air before the hunters caught them. The priestesses signal sounded much further away, and Alissa wondered if her lungs could handle a longer swim with the drum still shaking her insides, but knowing they were being pursued left her with no other choice. They inhaled deeply then swam for the sound of the priestess, however this time she wasn't whistling, but chanting. It was a familiar tune, the same she sang for Alissa when the young woman worried she couldn't cross the river of disease. They popped up in a small cavern glowing with the faint green light of the phosphorescent moss. The shadow woman stood on the jagged rocks of the bank of the hidden pool. Alissa gasped for air, her chest felt constricted. She hardly had the strength to climb out of the cenote waters. Wes helped push her up onto the black rocks before he dragged himself out to sit beside of her.

In the faint green glow Alissa looked at him. Wes's skin was blue, riddled with lacerations. He pushed his hair out of his face and she could see his arm was crooked with a fractured bone. It was his eyes that sent a shock to her heart, it felt worse than when the ritual drum pounded when she realized they were clouded over.

"Wes," she wept.

He knew the reason she cried. The truth he couldn't bring himself to reveal to her since the moment they realized they had stepped into Xibalba. Grief sickened him when his eyes scanned her stained skin, gashes on her wrists, and white, lifeless lips. He stood up, holding out his hand to her.

"Let's go," he said.

"Why are we fighting so hard?" she asked.

He didn't know how to answer her so he just kept his hand outstretched, waiting for her to take it. Alissa knew in her heart if she were to make it beyond the elaborate door it would not matter, because she was nothing more than a corpse.

"We are dead already, right?" Alissa asked.

"Pretty close to it," he answered.

She looked up at him, and he was waiting for her. "Let's go."

"Why?" She cried as she put her cold hand in his.

"Because, if this is going to end, then it is going to be done our way and not his," Wes said.

Wes helped her take the pack off of her shoulders, then held it up before her. They looked to each other, both knowing what was hidden at the bottom of the dripping backpack. Alissa stared into his eyes, the eyes of a corpse, and nodded. She knew what he had planned, and she just hoped they had the time to do it. The priestess understood the meaning of the silent agreement. She beckoned to them and they followed her with new determination.

The Wayobs came splashing up into the small chamber filled with green light. The humans were nowhere to be seen, yet they left the stink of failing bodies behind. The hunters spoke in their own guttural tongue. The stronger of the two dove back into the cenote water while the others tracked the prey down the long-hidden passageway, making his way as quickly as he could to close the gap between them.

Ah-Puch was standing at the lip of the cenote, his legions screaming rabidly as they awaited the Wayobs return. The Lord of Death knew the mischief maker had intervened when he saw the group of Skeleton Coats coming to the defense of the humans. Shadow Priestess had long been a thorn in his side, one he hoped to extricate. The shaman behind him was lost in the beating of the ritual drum, yet his demon lieges came to whisper into his ear. Revolt was in the air; it had permeated the lands of fear like the stink of plague corpses for centuries. The priestess had to be dealt with, and it would show the skeleton tribe to get back in line as well. Ah-Puch called forth Blood Bringer then instructed him to summon his daughter, Blood Maiden, the eater of energy. She was the only one cunning enough to capture a shadow.

CHAPTER TWENTY

Wes and Alissa had to push themselves to keep up with Shadow Priestess, who moved quickly down the hidden passageway. The drum still thundered, as even in the bowels of the mountain it found the hearts of the humans. Alissa stumbled over a loose stone and fell hard. The shadow woman paused to give them time to catch up to her, after Wes had helped Alissa back onto her feet. They continued at the same relentless pace. The sense of urgency Shadow Priestess radiated kept them on edge. The pathway began to gradually narrow until they were forced to crawl through the darkness. A familiar sound came echoing from behind them, mocking them as they scrambled faster.

****

Skeleton Queen's spy returned reporting the humans had not resurfaced and a handful of her warriors had perished in the cenote. She was confident the Shadow Priestess had intervened. The simian ruler gathered a group of her warriors and sent the rest of her people into the caverns to hide. She led her small army to the decaying city, its buildings nothing more than crypts and tombstones. Skeleton Queen knew of the only passageway the priestess could use to escape the Lord of Xibalba, it ended in the floor of a ruined mausoleum. She had no idea what the priestess had planned after emerging from the tunnels, but she meant to defend her against the ravenous inhabitants of the city of rot. The soldiers stalked silently along with their queen through the dead forest, keen to any movement or sounds about them. They quickly found cover at the sounds of the owl men above. The queen dispatched two sentries to survey the Wayob who passed over quickly. They scaled a corpse tree in a matter of seconds to see the hunters flying in the direction of the forest beyond the river of sickness. They nimbly descended to report to the queen. She knew the mistress of the wood and the creature she kept, something in her gut told her it was a bad omen. She hailed her troops, and ordered them onward with all haste. The atmosphere in the land of fear was much darker, it alarmed the Skeleton Queen.

****

The Wayob hooted. It wanted to tease them with its presence. He knew they were close, could smell them near. It got down on its hands and knees to crawl through the shrinking tunnel. Its abnormal form was not of a natural creature, and though it was strong it was also uncoordinated when trying to maneuver nimbly.

Its eyes were attuned to seeing in darkness, and ahead of itself caught a glimpse of the young man. He was stuck in a tight spot in the tunnel, fighting to squeeze through. The Wayob's face twisted into a satisfied grin. He hooted once more. His prey scrambled in terror, screaming as his skin was torn away from having to force himself between the jagged rock walls.

****

Ah-Puch silenced the jeering crowd as the Wayob emerged from the blue maw. He knew the significance of the creature returning alone. The hunter dreaded reporting to the master, and it was obvious in the way it cowered before him. The humans had eluded them, yet they could not forever with the second Wayob still on their trail, and it would drag them both back to the Lord of Xibalba by the hair of their heads.

Ah-Puch and his lieges headed up the macabre train as they exited the ritual cavern and made their way to the pyramid temple to await the Blood Maiden. The inflamed crowd of walking corpses was instructed to hunt the humans. Ah-Puch would not rest until the ritual was complete, when he could add their hearts to his wall and their staggering corpses to his loyal legion.

****

The priestess whistled frantically. Alissa helped Wes along, his abdomen and back flayed open from the tooth-like stones. The tunnel was opening up, allowing them to stand once more and run. The Wayob growled furiously as he became stuck in the very spot Wes left his flesh behind. It bought them the time to put more ground between them and the hunter. The passage intersected two other tunnels, and the priestess ran tirelessly for the one veering to the right-hand side.

Alissa halted beside the shadow woman who stood beneath a square hole shedding soft, green light down on her. The priestess pointed up, indicating their exit. Wes hoisted Alissa up and she climbed onto the dusty floor of a small stone building. She immediately turned back to drag Wes up as he jumped to grab the ledge of the hole and pull himself to freedom of the hidden tunnel. The shadow priestess came climbing into the room effortlessly.

They looked around them and saw patches of moss growing inside the empty mausoleum, lighting it like a jack-o'-lantern from the inside. Shadow Priestess whistled for them to follow her as she slipped down the center of the silent burial chamber. They stopped before the opened doorway, and beyond it torchlight shown upon the crumbled facades of the city. Alissa thought it looked like a massive graveyard, as broken crypts lined the cobbled street. Shadow Priestess stepped out into the city of the dead and the humans followed.

****

They could hear the ragged wailing of the putrid inhabitants of the city returning. They hurried along, keeping themselves hidden among the ruins. The throngs followed the Lord of Death as he and his kings convened at the Pyramid temple, and the shaman followed, beating the drum obediently. Wayobs were sent to search from above while the mass of blue-skinned ghouls scattered at the command of Ah-Puch. Wes gripped Alissa's hand. The doorway could be seen, not close enough to make a run for it yet, but still within reach. The constant thrumming intensified with the ritual drum being so close, and it slowed Alissa down. She gripped her chest, and fear came with the agony of it. Wes wrapped her arm over his shoulder trying to guide her but he was wracked with exhaustion. Alissa dragged Wes down with her as she fell, with the sudden impact with the cracked stone floor causing her to scream, a short yelp of penned up terror. The shadow priestess kept on moving hurriedly, darting into the cover of a fallen pillar. A shrill cry from above told the priestess they were spotted.

A rasping growl was followed by talons puncturing Wes's side as the Wayob came down on top of them. In the distance a chorus of hungry shrieks echoed through the decrepit city.

Shadow Priestess heard the attack, turning to see the humans being assaulted. She ran to them in desperation and cursed the creature. A small horde was also coming for them, creeping quickly towards Wes and Alissa.

Alissa kicked at the owl man as he bent over to grab Wes by the hair. The blow connected, yet had little effect. She rolled over and pushed herself up onto her feet. She leaped upon the back of the hunter as he tried lifting Wes into the air. Alissa raked her fingernails across the enlarged eye of the Wayob. It squawked and screeched, releasing Wes, and it flipped her over its back. Alissa landed on her back, stunned yet able to fight. It clawed at her face, then grabbed her by the throat, pinning her to the ground in its powerful grip. Wes picked up a piece of the rubble littering the broken road beside him, and he used it to bludgeon the beast in the back of its head. It let go of Alissa, then flew above them squawking angrily, and darted away. They knew it was going to report to the Lord of Death. The group of putrid minions of Xibalba would be on them in a matter of minutes. Suddenly, squeaking from the tops of the dilapidated buildings told them the skeleton coats had come to their rescue. The little warriors came wielding rocks and debris, throwing it down onto the dried-out walking corpses.

Shadow priestess hailed them, and Alissa and Wes ran as more of the dead approached.

****

The Wayob landed upon the pyramid steps to report it had seen the humans, just as its brothers arrived with the Blood Maiden and her creature. The Nagual was blindfolded, as the blue torchlight would have frightened the beast. The sorceress came to aid her father and the master in retrieving the humans, specifically the girl who left her blind. The maiden's face was never beautiful, but now it was marred with seeping blisters, both of her eyes sealed shut. She was sightless yet approached her father as if her eyes could see clearly. He lifted a calloused hand to her scorched countenance and promised she could cut out Alissa's eyes if she succeeded. Ah-Puch ordered the Wayob to carry the sorceress and her companion to the humans.

****

They were attacked by the second group of the dead. Among them was Professor Lipton, who came hobbling along on his shattered legs. Wes refused to run from him, but he turned back, and picked up a loose brick from the broken roof of a low tomb beside him. The old professor came for Wes; his face was devoid of the friendly caring it once held for his associate professor. It was filled with hunger and hatred. Wes brought the brick up then slammed the old man in the side of his head. He writhed on the ground before attempting to rise. Wes used the brick like a hammer to smash Professor Lipton over the head again, then across his back, and finally across his broken shins. One of the professor's bones popped free, leaving him scrambling to stand as Wes ran to catch up to shadow woman and Alissa as they approached the doorway. The skeleton coats rushed in with more ferocity, using rocks and teeth and claws to rend the dry corpses apart.

CHAPTER TWENTY-ONE

They waited for him at the bottom of the stone steps leading up to the antechamber. The way into it was still teeming with vampiric vines, hungry to sink their thorns into the veins of the humans. Alissa's body was so tortured she only wished for death. She wanted an end to it all. She kept repeating to herself what Wes told her in the cenote tunnel. If it was going to end, it would end her way. She refused to become one of the fiends pursuing them, so death would come by her own hands. She looked to the priestess, the brave woman who chose the same end centuries before, and saw the shadow stood proud and unyielding. It strengthened her for what she had to do.

Wes fell at the foot of the stairs, his lungs crying for air. His entire body was a raw nerve; pain had become him. He rose shakily, pulled the pack from his back, and removed the disc. He gripped it in one blood-crusted hand, then ascended the steps, taking Alissa by his other hand.

****

The priestess could see them coming. The winged hunters carried two figures, searching among the fighting between the skeleton coats and the underworld creatures. It wouldn't be long until they were pointed in her direction. She knew the sorceress remembered her, and how Blood Maiden had nearly drained her of all of her energy. Shadow Priestess readied herself as the Wayobs screeched and headed their way. She strode forward to greet them.

****

The shaman continued to drum as the Lord of Death paced before him. The ritual was underway, both humans were already marked to die. There was no way they could walk in the land of the living again. The rhythm was dying slowly like the beating of a heart over a lifetime, gradually losing its strength and fading away. The time was coming when it would stop completely.

****

Wes and Alissa stood at the top step together, but the chamber could not be seen through the tangle of creepers. The thirsty vines came creeping along the ground, twining around the legs of Alissa and Wes, sinking barbs into their flesh. It was like getting caught in barbed wire; the finality of it sank in on them. Alissa squeezed his hand tightly, tears fell down her cheeks.

"We can do this together," Wes said.

"We have to," Alissa agreed.

She nodded, then pulled him forward. They became swallowed up by the sanguinary tentacles of the plant.

****

The Wayobs softly deposited the sorceress upon the ground with the Nagual beside her. She could not see the priestess with her scorched eyes, yet she could feel her energy strongly. Blood Maiden hissed as the priestess approached. The Nagual was still blindfolded, but the outskirts of the dead city were much darker than the torch-lined street so she slid it from the beast's eyes. It turned its reptilian face towards the shadow priestess, then bared its jagged, black teeth. The Blood Maiden laughed, a lilting laughter like that of the deranged, before bringing her hand up, pointing at the shadow woman, and she spoke a language more ancient than even the dialect of the priestess. It was the tongue of the gods. The power of the spell she was preparing to cast was like a gathering storm. Electricity popped in the cavern air. Her voice began as a rasping string of repetitive words, then built into a wailing as winds kicked up around her. Shadow Priestess had witnessed a force similar, yet not as strong, only once, the first time she became a victim of the blood maiden. She refused to flee. It would leave Wes and Alissa open to an attack and they needed to focus on sealing the doorway once more. The Blood Maiden cast out a net of energy, like a spider web, and it wrapped around the shadow priestess, leaving her helpless while the blood maiden fed. The witch cackled then nodded down to her pet as she reached into a sack at her waist to toss it a handful of bloodied entrails. The Nagual stalked up to dine before the shadow priestess, its reptilian face blank as it sought any spirits connected to the shadow woman.

****

The thorns were embedded deeply in their flesh, suckling from their blood. Wes and Alissa struggled to keep moving; nothing mattered anymore as long as they had the strength left to drag the door closed and then seal it again for all eternity. As the drum died so did they, and something insidious threatened to force its way to the surface. Wes could feel it, a blossoming violence, and that it would consume them and leave them hollow and hungry for the flesh of the living. The thought of becoming a monster, of Alissa withering into a vile scavenger feeding on carrion like a vulture, enraged him. He thrust his body through the raking, clinging thorns. It burned like acid as his skin came away. Half of his face was nothing but raw flesh, and his arms, torso, and legs were nearly skinned completely as he yanked himself free of the vines. It receded, greedily coveting the large chunks of his skin before winding tighter around the young woman, refusing to release her. Wes laid the disc down beside the doorway, then returned to grip her cold white hands in his, but they were slick with his own blood, making it hard for him to keep a hold of her. She was dreadfully weak, her eyes lulled shut as the arms of the thorny plant held her. A barb was embedded in her left eye, another pierced through her lip pulling it up away from her teeth. She whimpered as Wes struggled to free her and keep himself from being coiled up in them again.

****

The Nagual's face morphed into a familiar visage; it wept and held its throat. It took on the appearance of one of the worker boys who helped her seal the door. In a tiny voice it spoke to her then, accusing her of murder. It asked if she enjoyed dragging a blade over its throat. The vision was saddening, yet she knew the trickster was only trying to fill her with more sorrow and despair before feasting upon her. The first time she became ensnared by Mistress of the Wood the Nagual took the shape of a young woman, who the priestess acted as a midwife to, and she died asking if her stillborn babe would live. The Blood Maiden concentrated on the web as she opened her mouth wide, it lurched wider, unhinging like the jaws of a snake. Shadow woman felt her energy being sapped. She would soon be completely consumed. She cried out in desperation.

****

Skeleton Queen's army suffered a great loss, but the dead were being held back. She felt an electricity building in the atmosphere, like a thunderstorm gathering around them. A scream caught her attention, and glancing to the source of it she could see the witch had the priestess bound in a powerful spell. She screeched to a group of her warriors, frantically seeking some way to distract the sorceress before she devoured the shadow woman whole.

****

Alissa's hand slid out of Wes's. The vines had a strong hold on her, plunging its thorns into every inch of her flesh. He tried again, grabbing her by the wrists as the insidious plant reached out to claim him once more. He trembled violently as he slapped them away, but the plant was growing stronger with the blood it took from them, becoming far too powerful to battle against.

****

The Nagual was lost in pretending to be the spirit of a worker boy when the skeleton coats attacked. They carried between them a blue-flamed torch, frightening the creature enough to cause it to run wildly into the darkness forgetting any loyalty it had towards the Blood Maiden. Skeleton Queen jumped onto the back of the sorceress, then sank her teeth into the neck of the witch. Her strong jaws tore a chunk from her enemy, and she spat the sooty flesh upon the ground, then went in for another mouthful. Blood Maiden spun, grabbing at the simian queen. The spell weakened as the sorceress turned her attention to battling the skeleton coats as they swarmed over her. Shadow Priestess managed to free herself from the cocoon of black magic around her as a screech of agony halted the fray. Blood Maiden held the Skeleton Queen's limp body in her hands, as the warrior queen's spine was broken in the battle. Her warriors redoubled their attack viciously, clawing and biting at the face and throat of the witch who killed their ruler. The skeleton coats crawled up her back, then lifted their torch and lit the back of her hair on fire. She wailed as the flames spread over her, then she retreated to the company of the other dead things who were left mangled by the army of tiny monkeys.

Shadow Priestess ordered them to carry the torch to the vines covering the antechamber, then she bent over the body of her closest friend. The Skeleton Queen died as she had lived, doing the honorable thing. She was the closest thing to a human in the lands of fear the priestess had encountered in centuries of dwelling here, far more so than those who were once human themselves.

****

A blue glow shone through the mess of tangled vines. The tentacles shrank back and withered as flames fed hungrily upon the plant. The blue fire swept over Alissa who was still bound tightly in the plant as it bled her nearly dry. The fire devoured her hair and burned her skin, yet she was free at last. Wes and Alissa could feel their hearts stammering, and the drum would soon reverberate through their bodies for the last time. They gripped the circular openings in the doors and began pulling with the remainder of their strength. The stone doors moved slowly as Wes and Alissa towed them back into place. Shadow Priestess ordered the skeleton coats to stand on each other's shoulders to hold the disc in place.

Alissa lifted the dagger from the shadow woman's remains, and then held it out to Wes as the priestess began her chant, using the same prayer she did many years before when she and the young boys spilled their own blood upon the door, sealing their own tomb. Alissa looked like a corpse, Wes knew he did too. The fear in her eyes was gone, a weary want for release remained. He placed his skinless hand against her charred cheek, and with one last caress he plunged the dagger into her heart. She exhaled deeply, but never drew breath again. Wes eased her down onto the chamber floor before the entryway. Her blood flowed towards it, and then began to climb up the etched stone door. The priestess was deep in a ritualistic prayer, calling upon the old gods to seal off the lands of fear. Wes lifted the blade up, positioned it over his stammering heart, then drove in the dagger. He fell to his knees as he withdrew the sacrificial blade, and with the last beats of his heart his blood was forced out onto the elaborate hieroglyphics. They began to glow, and as he shut his eyes for the final time in his ravaged human body, he saw the disc shine brightly with their blood offering and a single pulse of white light filled the chamber.

****

Blood Maiden hailed one of the Wayobs who flew over surveying the damage to the master's legions. It came to her aid, lifting her up and baring her away to the temple while the inhabitants of Xibalba waged war against one another. The sorceress was smoldering when she was dropped atop the pyramid where Ah-Puch awaited news from his warriors. Blood King roared in frustration yet Master of Death stood with a face of stone. He lifted a hand and his men stopped their fuming to hear the drum being beaten for its last time. The humans could not evade him forever; he was certain of it. Only now it seemed they had all of eternity to try.

****

Wes's spirit lifted from the burden of his battered shell, and he felt stronger than he ever had, without the encumbrance of his broken body. The abuse he suffered at the hands of Ah-Puch and his monstrous legion was evident in the flesh he shed. It left a lingering hatred of them all. Alissa's silhouette waited beside the shadow woman who held her spectral hand over the young woman's face.

"She said we can move on whenever we choose," Alissa spoke.

"But I'm not finished here," he answered.

"Neither am I," she said.

It would now be whispered throughout, of the three shadows that roamed Xibalba seeking to thwart the Lord of Death.

THE END.

About The Authors

Melissa Lason and Michelle Garza have been writing together since they were little girls. Dubbed The Sisters of Slaughter by the editors of Fireside Press. They are constantly working together on new stories in the horror and dark fantasy genres. Their work has been included in FRESH MEAT published by Sinister Grin Press, WISHFUL THINKING by Fireside Press, and WIDOWMAKERS a benefit anthology of dark fiction.

https://facebook.com/sistersofhorror/

Coming Soon

Hell Hollow by Ronald Kelly

Lights Out by Nate Southard

Blister by Jeff Strand

Find these and other horrific books at sinistergrinpress.com